D0380078

LADY GOLD INVESTIGATES ~ VOLUME 2

COMPANION SHORT STORIES TO GINGER
GOLD MYSTERIES

LEE STRAUSS

la
plume
PRESS

THE CASE OF THE RECIPE ROBBERY

1

"*W*ouldn't that be something if we suddenly found ourselves sitting next to Gladys Cooper or Nancy Price?" Mrs. Ginger Reed, alias Lady Gold, couldn't help but glance around the dining room of *The Bromley*, a popular Soho restaurant, for a sign of a famous theatre or film star. She and her husband, Chief Inspector Basil Reed, opened up the menus that the waiter had given them, as she continued, "Did you know they're filming a new motion picture in London?"

"What on earth would I gain from sitting next to some celebrity?" Basil said with a broad smile and a glint in his hazel eyes. He leaned forward as if telling a secret. "I have you here to outshine them all, my love."

"You do know how to flatter a girl." Ginger couldn't help the small blush that rose to her cheeks. Newly married, her handsome husband still had that effect on her.

They both ordered the same dish, *gigot d'agneau* — French roast leg of lamb — and the head chef's version of *pommes dauphine*. Ginger chose a pinot noir to go with the lamb dish while Basil ordered an Italian Chianti.

Ginger marvelled at how it was so easy to spend time

with Basil. There were rarely uncomfortable, silent spaces, indeed if there was a silent moment it was altogether comfortable, with neither feeling the need to speak. Then, in the next moment they could be talking about things that were close to the heart and important to them both.

The Bromley featured gold and cream wallpaper, vaulted ceilings, and thick red carpeting, which kept the ambient conversation noise at a comfortable level so that even when the restaurant was busy, it was easy to have a quiet conversation. Ginger knew that the restaurant had been a favourite of Londoners for a very long time, due in part to the varied cuisine, which was always delicious.

"The head chef is known for his original and innovative recipes for both international and British fare," Basil said, taking a sip of his wine. "I've heard that celebrities like E. M. Forster and Agatha Christie sometimes come here, and I once saw Tom Walls—you know, the actor— when I was here with a work colleague."

"Impressive," Ginger remarked. She actually didn't like Tom Walls' acting but she kept that to herself in order not to dampen Basil's enthusiasm.

"Perhaps we could even go and see a late performance at The Prince's Theatre, after this," Basil said. "Noël Coward's latest production, *Hay Fever, i*s running there right now, I think."

Ginger patted her lips with a linen napkin and pushed a strand of red hair behind one ear. "Marvellous idea, love." She wore a mauve crepe Georgette evening dress embroidered with large silver pearls, and draped at the side with three ribbons in different shades of purple. It was perfectly suited for a night on the town.

Basil had just asked the waiter for the bill when the reserved atmosphere was abruptly disturbed.

"Zees ees outrageous!" A distinguished-looking middle-aged man across the room suddenly stood, and dramatically threw his napkin onto his plate of unfinished food. "I will not stand for zees. It has gone too far!" The Frenchman's face flushed with anger as he glared towards the kitchen. He was tall and slender with black hair that was smoothed back on his head, a long, thin nose, a full moustache, and sideburns.

The maître d', a dour man wearing the attire of a head waiter, rushed over. "Dear sir, how can I help you?"

"I demand to speak to your chef. Where ees he?" The offended man's Adam's apple bounced. "How dare he! I have been robbed. Zees ees a crime!"

A shock rippled through the crowd. A lady sitting near Ginger said to her husband, "That's Marcel Arseneault! The famous *chef de cuisine*!"

Monsieur Arseneault couldn't be quieted and wouldn't allow himself to be led out of the room. He seemed intent on making an embarrassing scene while everyone stared in shock. "Zees is robbery of zee worst kind!"

Ginger and Basil rose from their chairs at the same time, shared a questioning look, then turned quickly towards the angry man and the flustered maître d'.

The man opened his mouth to shout again, but Basil interrupted him. "Now look here, I'm Chief Inspector Basil Reed of Scotland Yard. I cannot permit you to keep yelling, sir. This is a public place and furthermore a place of business. I can arrest you on the grounds of causing a disturbance."

The man sputtered but did not seem capable of forming a sentence. "Well I…I… that ees to say… I'm…"

Ginger turned to the maître d'. "Is there a private room somewhere close?" She couldn't help but be thoroughly curious, and wanted to give the man an opportunity to explain himself.

The maître d', clearly relieved that someone had taken charge, nodded. "Right this way."

They were led to a smaller version of the main dining

room. "This area is reserved for private functions," he explained. "I will fetch Mr. Chatsworth, the chef, at once."

He closed the double glass doors behind him and they sat at the nearest table to wait.

The protester drew a deep breath. "I am zee great chef Marcel Louis Arseneault! I will not tolerate zees humiliation, and I demand…"

"Sir," Basil said, cutting him off. "Please, state clearly the nature of your complaint."

"Zee problem ees outright thievery of the worst kind!"

"Did someone steal your wallet or something else of value?" Basil asked, leaning forward in his chair. "If so, I will need to make a report immediately and search the premises."

"No, nothing trivial like zat. Zees is something far more nefarious."

Ginger prompted, "Do continue."

"A *recette*." The man threw up his hands. "A recipe! *Rata-touille* to be exact. A dish from zee south-east of France."

Basil and Ginger looked at each other with raised eyebrows.

"I'm afraid I don't understand," Basil said. "There are likely to be many ways to cook that dish. How do you know someone stole your recipe?"

"From zee taste!" The man started waving his right hand wildly at his mouth. "Yes, zees is a favourite dish but I have concocted a recipe zat ees very distinct and depends on zee exact length of time you must sauté zee vegetables and by adding certain extra herbs to normal ingredients of tomatoes, garlic, onions, courgette, aubergine…" He counted on his fingers.

Ginger cut him off, "Yes, but do you mean to say you are convinced of theft because of the *taste*?"

"But of course." Monsieur Arseneault stared at Ginger incredulously. "And who are you?"

6

Basil answered on Ginger's behalf. "This is my wife, Mrs. Reed."

"*Enchanté.*" He shook her hand and bowed slightly. "So back to your question, Mrs. Reed. I know my own creations, just as surely as a father would know ees own children! To make eet worse, zees ees not zee only one! I have tasted counterfeits of several of my other dishes at various 'fine' restaurants all over zees city in zee last few weeks." He said the word 'fine' with much sarcasm. Basil and Ginger shared another amused look.

"From a police perspective, Monsieur Arseneault," Basil said, "I'm afraid that isn't good evidence that a crime has been committed. Your sense of taste is not going to be enough to convince a judge in any court that I can think of. How do you know someone did not just taste your dish and sought to duplicate the results?"

Monsieur Arseneault rolled his eyes. "Zees ees simply not possible. No one is zat talented, not even me." The chef vigorously tapped his chest with his finger. "And in addition to zees, zeese recipes have not been released. Zey are unpublished so to speak. No one except for myself and my assistant have tasted zem."

Just then the maître d' entered the room along with a middle-aged portly man in chef's whites. "May I introduce the head chef here, Mr. Chatsworth."

Mr. Chatsworth, who seemed to be in his fifties, had sandy hair which was slightly tousled from having just removed his chef's hat. He wore spectacles, which made his intense, bright-blue eyes seem larger than usual, and watched in horror as his opponent rose suddenly from his chair and waved his fists in front of himself in a boxing stance.

"I will claim my honour. You mountebank...you charlatan! En garde!" the Frenchman yelled.

"I say, old chap," began Mr. Chatsworth as he took a step back and raised his own fists in defence, a wild, astonished look on his face, "I don't know what you're on about but if it's fisticuffs you want..." He frantically waved his clenched hands in front of his face, pausing only to push his spectacles back up on his nose.

Ginger had to hide her face behind her hands for fear of letting out a chuckle at this absurd display of chefs' bravado. Nonetheless, she was glad she didn't have to be the one to break it up.

"I will have none of this!" shouted Basil as he rose from his chair. "Mr. Arseneault, I will not warn you again!" The two chefs stared at each other. "Sit. Down!" Basil said forcefully.

Monsieur Arseneault risked a sideways glance at Basil, then slowly sat back down.

Having regained control of the room, Basil tugged on his waistcoat. "You, Mr. Chatsworth, please sit over there."

Mr. Chatsworth complied and claimed a chair on the opposite side of the table, out of the reach of the agitated Frenchman.

"Now then," Basil said. "I want the simplest and the quickest route to the truth here."

"He stole my recipe!" The Frenchman glared across the table.

"I didn't steal any bloody recipe," Mr. Chatsworth said. He folded thick arms over his chest, huffing a bit, rather out of breath.

"You are a liar," Monsieur Arseneault sputtered, his Adam's apple bobbing.

Mr. Chatsworth bounced in his chair. "And you are a fool!"

Basil stretched out his arms in warning. "Gentlemen, this may not be a matter for the police, but it certainly will be if you don't remain calm."

Ginger held out a hand to Mr. Chatsworth. "I'm Mrs. Reed. I found your leg of lamb to be delightful."

The chef shot the Frenchman a sharp glance before smiling back at Ginger. "I regret that your dining experience has been needlessly ruined. Please be my guest the next time you decide to dine here."

Monsieur Arseneault harrumphed.

Basil pressed on. "I feel compelled to inform you that Mrs. Reed runs an office as a private detective."

At this, both chefs raised their eyebrows and looked at Ginger from a new perspective.

"She is jolly good at what she does and … even though I don't know if she would agree to become involved," he said, nodding at Ginger, "I daresay, Monsieur Arseneault, you may want to enquire about her services in this matter."

"Oh? Why ees zat?"

"Because this is a very strange situation," Basil said. "A police matter involves a crime that is provable in court."

"I have not committed any crime," Mr. Chatsworth said.

"Be that as it may," continued Basil, "even if you had, there would be no way to prove it. I'm not about to order a police constable to watch over you as you cook, and if you had a written copy of the recipe I am sure you could hide it, or destroy it even before we were able to look for it."

"That is absurd," Mr. Chatsworth said.

Monsieur Arseneault slapped a hand on the table and leaned in. "Where did you get your recipe for *ratatouille?*"

Mr. Chatsworth met him halfway, fists pressing against the tabletop, and Ginger feared their noses would knock together. "That is none of your business!" the chef said, "but I can certainly tell you that I did not steal it from you!" Mr. Chatsworth then turned to Basil. "Chief Inspector Reed, I assume that I have the right to refuse service to anyone whom I deem to be causing a disturbance in my place of business?"

Basil let out a sigh. "Yes, I suppose that is correct."

"Well then, if you are not conducting an investigation at the moment, and I am not under arrest, then I am going to return to my very busy kitchen. In the meantime, as an officer of the law, and as a witness to this man disrupting the peace in my restaurant, I adjure you to kindly escort this man out of my restaurant." At this, he stood up and walked resolutely out of the room.

Basil, Ginger, and Monsieur Arseneault sat looking at each other for a moment.

"I cannot believe zat you cannot do anything about zees." Monsieur Arseneault shook his head and looked helplessly at Basil.

"I am very sorry," Basil returned, "but the man is within his rights."

Monsieur Arseneault turned to Ginger. "It seems you are my last hope in zees matter. Would you agree to help me? I will pay any reasonable fee."

"I am not entirely sure," Ginger said. "As my husband has already said, this is a puzzle that would be difficult to solve since the very fact that any theft has taken place is in question. You must admit, Monsieur Arseneault, your sense of taste, while highly esteemed, is not the strongest proof for anyone else who does not share your... culinary sensitivity. "

"Please, Mrs. Reed, zeese recipes are like treasures of gold. Zey are supposed to be published in a new recipe book at the end of zees year by Bowes Publishing, one of England's largest publishers. Zis ees a follow-up to a very successful book I published last year. You may have seen it, *French Cooking for English Kitchens*."

Ginger had indeed heard about this famous book. *The London Times* had called it "a revolution in international cookery". It went against societal norms in London, which regarded talking about food as being rather inappropriate. A well-known quote from the book was "*food worth eating is food worth talking about*".

"Yes, I have heard of that book," replied Ginger. "It made quite a splash last year."

"Zee anticipation for a follow-up book ees quite impressive. I am working on it now with an English collaborator to deliver it to zee publishers on time. But now zat some of zeese recipes have already been prematurely revealed, it ruins all prospects of a successful book release. I will be made *un objet de risée*, a mockery."

"I'm afraid I don't understand. Wouldn't it just be good promotion for your book if people tasted the recipes before the book was published?" Ginger asked.

"Yes, if I was credited with zee recipe perhaps, but as you can see zeese chefs do not intend to give me credit for zose recipes. Zerefore I am made to look like a fraud, claiming to be zee originator of zeese fantastic dishes after zey are already on menus all over London. Besides, I want to be in control of how and when my recipes are introduced into zee world. It is a great matter of principle!"

Ginger let out a long breath and after a moment of thought opened her handbag. "Here's my card. Please set up an appointment with my assistant and we can discuss this further."

2

*A*s he sat across from Ginger's desk in the office of Lady Gold Investigations, Monsieur Arseneault seemed a bit calmer then he had the night before. His tall frame filled the leather-backed chair as he glanced around the office at the gold and beige papered walls, plush red carpet, and Ginger's fine walnut desk. Felicia Gold, Ginger's sister-in-law by her first marriage, a thoroughly modern young lady, sat at the adjacent desk, ready to take notes. Boss, Ginger's Boston terrier, was lying in his usual place, a wicker basket next to Ginger's desk, gnawing on a dog treat.

The Frenchman peered down at Boss with a look of amusement. "My wife, Flora, also has a dog zat she loves. It ees a French bulldog she calls 'François'. François has a particular penchant for French pastry, I'm afraid, so he ees needing a rather large basket since he does not fit in zee normal one anymore. He ees also sneezing all zee time, it seems to me. I only tolerate zee pudgy leetle dog, but my wife adores heem." Monsieur Arseneault's pronounced Adam's apple bobbed slightly as he took a sip of his tea.

The thought of a sneezing, plump French bulldog made

both Felicia and Ginger smile. Ginger felt a bit more comfortable with her decision to take the case. Unlike his performance at *The Bromley*, the French chef seemed rather reasonable today, and the thought of this case affecting the high society culinary world of London intrigued her.

"Well, let's start with some basic questions, shall we?" Ginger began. "When did you start realising your recipes had been stolen?"

"One month ago, I was dining with my wife at a restaurant on Sheraton Street. I ordered zee *poulet chasseur* because I had recently perfected a beautiful combination of ingredients for zee reduced *chasseur* sauce. I was curious to compare zem. Imagine my horror when I immediately recognised zee distinctive taste zat I had just invented in my own private kitchen! It is a far more bold and exciting taste zan zee normal sauces for zees dish, especially when paired with zee right French wine. In any case my wife also tasted it and we both agreed. It was my own recipe!"

"Did you enquire in the kitchen?" Felicia said as she looked up from her notes.

"But of course. The man simply refused to tell me where he got it from. Since zen, I visited ten more of zee finer restaurants in Soho, trying various French dishes. At five of zem I recognised my own creations. Each time zee chef refused to let me know where he got hees recipe."

Monsieur and Madame Arseneault had done a lot of fine dining recently, Ginger thought. She turned to Felicia. "Please make sure you get the list of these restaurants before Monsieur Arseneault leaves." She turned back to the chef, "I am assuming you have all of your recipes written down somewhere?"

He nodded dramatically. "Yes, naturally I have zem all recorded. I create zees dishes in my private kitchen and record everything in a large notebook which is kept hidden in a safe. Zees is done in French but ees later translated into English by my publishers, of course."

"Sounds all very scientific," Felicia remarked.

"It ees more like creating art," Monsieur Arseneault replied. "But zere is an element of *chimie* involved of course." He nodded politely at Felicia.

"Who is the first person other than yourself to taste each new recipe?" Ginger asked.

"My wife of course, she likes to taste and I value her opinion very much, but zere is also my former protégé. Hees name is Will Kendrick. However, I fired heem a few months ago."

"What can you tell me about him?" Ginger asked.

Monsieur Arseneault shrugged his shoulders. "He ees a tolerable cook. He was enthusiastic and I had initially had some hope zat he would someday show some brilliance as a chef. But sadly, as time went on it was obvious zat he did not have zee spark of innovation and had very little imagination. I had to let heem go."

"I see," Ginger said. "Did Mr. Kendrick aid you in the creation of these new recipes?"

"No, in addition to training him in zee art of general cookery, I only trained him to cook my recipes zat have already been made public. Specifically zose from my last book. However, I did ask him to taste each recipe alongside my wife. They both acted as my test subjects so to speak." He looked directly at Ginger. "My new recipes are created in isolation, I can assure you of zees, madame."

Ginger glanced at Felicia, who was busy taking notes, then asked, "How did Mr. Kendrick react when you let him go?"

"I know what you are thinking. When I informed him I did not wish to work with him, he walked out without even a word. He was upset, but frankly I believe zees young man is quite incapable of doing such a sing as zees. He lacks imagination. Trust me, I am a good judge of someone's character. Besides, he definitely did not have access to my safe. He does not even know where it ees."

"So you have not confronted him on this issue?" Ginger said.

"No, I have had no contact with him since I let him go and I would rather not have any in zee future, madame."

The chef certainly had confidence in his ability to read people, Ginger thought. "Is it possible for Miss Gold and me to view your kitchen and the room where you keep your safe?"

"But of course, you are welcome in our home."

"Thank you. Miss Gold will ring to make an appointment with you or your wife." Ginger pressed the tips of her manicured fingernails together and leaned forward in her chair. "Monsieur Arseneault, is there anyone you can think of who would wish you ill? Perhaps other restaurateurs in London?"

"*Non*, I cannot imagine!"

"Every criminal has a motive," Ginger replied smoothly, "and yet we have not established one in this case. We must discover who would gain from exposing your creations prematurely." Despite Monsieur Arseneault's shock at the idea, Ginger was guessing that with the Frenchman's expressive personality, his relatively quick success, and his excitable temperament, he had quite likely gained a measure of ill will amongst London's community of restaurateurs.

The chef stroked his full moustache and furrowed his eyebrows, deep in thought.

"You must have already thought of this," Ginger prompted. "Someone must have a reason, however ill-advised, to sabotage your ongoing successes."

"Yes, my wife and I have had several discussions about zees," Monsieur Arseneault said finally. "I am by nature a very agreeable man."

Ginger's face remained impassive at this peculiar assessment. Felicia hid a smirk behind her palm, but the Frenchman did not seem to notice.

"It ees hard for me to imagine that anyone would want to do zees since I am well loved everywhere I go."

3

*W*illiam Kendrick, Monsieur Arseneault's former protégé, proved difficult to track down. Monsieur Arseneault had given them an address and a physical description, but when Ginger and Felicia had arrived at the building in the Edgware district where they were met with a very irritable landlord. He informed them that the young man shared a flat with another fellow of about the same age and that they were both, in his estimation, "feckless laggards" who were constantly behind in their rent and having difficulty keeping gainful employment.

"They are quite a pair, those two," the severe-looking man remarked. "They're birds of the same feather, even though one of 'em is as French as the Eiffel Tower. I told me wife, Maggie, only yesterday that both of them blokes are more scared of 'ard work than the devil is of Easter Morning! One calls 'isself a photographer; the chemicals smell up the place somethin' awful. And the other says 'e's some sort of cook."

The landlord gave Ginger the address of a restaurant where he thought Mr. Kendrick might be working, but upon arrival, Ginger and Felicia were told that the young man had in fact only lasted a few weeks there, and he was now believed to be working during the hours of three and midnight at another restaurant called *The Guillotine*. Ginger and Felicia, with Boss happily relegated to the back seat, had just pulled up to *The Guillotine* in Ginger's 1924 Crossley when a young man exactly fitting the description Monsieur Arseneault had given, stepped outside and lit a cigarette. Will Kendrick wore stained chef's whites and carried his white cook's hat under his arm. His brown, tousled hair and unshaven face gave him a rather dishevelled look. Ginger guessed he was on a work break from the kitchen.

Ginger and Felicia stepped out of the motorcar.

"Excuse me," Ginger said. "I don't mean to be rude, but are you Mr. William Kendrick?"

Surprised, the fellow just stood and stared for a moment. "Y-yes, yes I am…"

"My name is Miss Felicia Gold," Felicia said, taking advantage of both the man's bafflement and her long fluttering eyelashes.

"I'm Mrs. Reed," Ginger said, turning towards Mr. Kendrick, "also known as Lady Gold from Lady Gold Investigations. We are looking into a matter for Mr. Arseneault, your former employer." Ginger watched the young man carefully as she said this. Her years working for the British Secret Service during the Great War had trained her to read people's facial expressions and body movements. Mr. Kendrick's eyes darted back and forth, and he looked rather uncomfortable at the mention of Arseneault's name.

"I am sure you wouldn't mind answering a few questions?" Felicia's inflection made the sentence sound like a question even though it was a statement. Her smile was radiant. The poor man didn't stand a chance, Ginger thought with a small smile.

The fellow's befuddlement was a good chance to be direct. "Monsieur Arseneault asserts that someone is stealing his new recipes and releasing them to various restaurants," Ginger stated. "Do you know anything about this?"

Mr. Kendrick took a long draught on his cigarette before throwing it on the ground and stepping on it. An effort to appear calm, Ginger thought. The cigarette had only just been lit.

"You think because he fired me that I'd look for some sort of revenge?"

Ginger stared back, unflinchingly. "Would you?"

"No! I'm not the type of person who does that sort of thing." He stared at his nicotine-stained fingers and then at the squashed cigarette at his feet with a modicum of regret. "I'm sure you've already spoken to Monsieur Arseneault or you wouldn't be here, so you know our history. Yes, he sacked me. No, I did not nick his recipes."

Mr. Kendrick produced another cigarette and lit it. "In fact, I wish Arseneault well. The man's a genius and deserves recognition."

Ginger detected sarcasm in his tone as he said the word "genius". His gaze darted between her and Felicia as he puffed on his cigarette. "I can tell you his personal style isn't easy to get along with, though. I was even a little bit relieved when he let me go, to be honest. He can jolly well find another apprentice to yell at as far as I'm concerned. I have more important things to do with my time." He glanced at the doorway and said, "Now if you'll excuse me, there's a *soupe à l'oignon* that needs my attention." He killed his second cigarette, then stepped into the building.

Felicia adjusted her hat. "Well, despite my formidable feminine wiles, I am not sure we gained much with that interview."

"On the contrary," Ginger replied as she opened the driver's door of the motorcar. "That conversation has told me one very interesting thing."

"That he's bitter?" Felicia asked.

Ginger started the motorcar and gave Boss a pat on the head. "That he is a young man with a secret."

4

*M*arcel and Flora Arseneault lived in a three-storey terraced red-brick house in Chelsea, which had once been famous for being the *borough of artists*. Many famous painters, writers, and so called "free thinkers" had lived in this area during the last part of the previous century and some still referred to it as the "bohemian district".

"Oscar Wilde lived around here," Ginger said, as she and Felicia climbed the four stone steps to the solid cherry-wood entrance door. Boss, tucked into Ginger's arms, peered about joyously. Felicia gazed down the street as if she hoped to catch sight of the famous Irish poet's ghost as Ginger, using the large brass doorknocker, tapped on the door.

"Bossy, you must be on your best behaviour today." Ginger stared affectionately into her dog's round brown eyes. "You are about to meet François and you must be civil. However, I don't want you getting any ideas about sharing his French pastry."

Ginger and Felicia shared a smile.

They were greeted by a slim, beautiful woman in her mid-forties. She had creamy, smooth skin, kind blue eyes surrounded by small wrinkles, and brown shingled hair that showed a bit of grey. She took in the trio with a dazzling smile, obviously delighted at the prospect of welcoming them into her home.

"*Mon Dieu*! My husband was right," she exclaimed. "You two ladies represent the epitome of fashion." She regarded Ginger and Felicia's outfits with wide, admiring eyes.

Oh mercy! Ginger thought. She liked this lady already.

"*Comme il est mignon!*" the lady said, her hands coming up to her cheeks. "What a beautiful dog!" She bent down and took Boss' head in both of her hands. Boss' tail stub wagged furiously.

"Oh, I am very sorry," their hostess said, her French accent muted. "Where are my manners? I am Madame Arseneault." She took Ginger's hand in both of hers and said, "You must be Mrs. Reed." Ginger smiled and nodded. She turned to Felicia. "And you are Miss Gold, yes?"

Felicia extended a gloved hand. "Pleased to meet you. Thanks so much for allowing us to come to your home."

The interior of the house was spacious and very modern. Mme Arseneault led them into a large parlour with rich, wooden panelling and beautiful leather and wood furniture. Just outside the entrance to the room there were stairways leading up to the other two floors.

"You have a very beautiful home," remarked Ginger, taking in the surroundings.

"Thank you, it was quite a job to renovate this one. When we arrived from Paris over twenty years ago, we bought two of the terraced houses side by side and made one large house. When we had our son, there was more than enough room for the three of us. This area is also perfect for our little family." Flora Arseneault smiled and gestured for them to take a seat. Just then the tall, slender figure of her husband entered the room followed by the most rotund French bulldog Ginger had ever seen.

François was similar in height to Boss, even though he had shorter legs. He shared Boss' short muzzle but was brown in colour and had a larger, more squarely shaped head with rounded tips on his ears rather than points. He sneezed twice, and then jauntily waddled over to Boss as if to welcome him to his home. Felicia's hand flew to her mouth to suppress a giggle. The two dogs exchanged the normal dog greeting of sniffing and tail wagging while all four humans looked on in amusement.

"Well now zat zees important *cérémonie* is finished," Monsieur Arseneault said with a broad smile, "let me welcome you to our humble home." He turned to his wife. "Flora, I do hope our maid has hidden away all of our pastries while we have another canine in our house?"

All three ladies chuckled at the small joke as they took a seat. François lay down on the plush carpet immediately in front of Boss who thought that was a wonderful idea and did the same.

"We don't mean to take up much of your time," Ginger said. "Since your home kitchen is the provenance of your recipes, I thought it wise to have a look. Naturally, we are still in the very beginnings of our investigation, but this seems like a good place to start."

At that moment, a young man in his twenties entered the room. The spitting image of Marcel Arseneault, he had the same slender nose, black hair, moustache, brown eyes, and lanky form, and most notably, the same bobbing Adam's apple.

" Zees is our son, Jean Claude. Jean Claude, meet Mrs. Reed and Miss Gold," Monsieur Arseneault said. The tall young man quickly walked over and politely shook Ginger's and Felicia's hands in turn.

"Pleased to meet you," he said. His gaze stayed on Felicia for a moment of admiration before he turned to his mother. "I am off to rehearsal, Maman."

"Well that is most fortunate, because it wouldn't do for you to be staring at our guest like some long-lost puppy." Mme Arseneault smiled warmly while shaking her head and raising her eyebrows.

Mr. Arseneault grinned at Felicia and said, "I hope this is not too forward, but if you like jazz music, please come to *the Lonely Street Cabaret* in Soho sometime. I play the piano in a trio and we perform there regularly. The place is really the bee's knees."

"We'll be sure to remember that," Ginger said, cutting in with a small, amused smile on her lips.

The young man turned to Ginger and blinked as if waking up from a dream. "Oh…, well, maybe I'll see you both there sometime."

"I don't know where zeese musicians come up with zeese strange words," Monsieur Arseneault remarked as the young man left the room. "Bee's knees?"

"It's American," Felicia offered.

"My son ees still trying to find heemself, I think," Monsieur Arseneault said. His tone indicated that there might be some tension between himself and the young man. "I often wonder what he would be like if he had a sibling." He shared a look with his wife. Ginger had the feeling that there was something unspoken that passed between them in that moment. "He has zee heart of an artist, but he puts all of his energies into zees new jazz music trend which will not last beyond next year. Such a waste." He shook his head for a moment, looking at the door, and then brightened up. "Would you like to view my kitchen now?"

5

"*I* know it ees unusual to have such a kitchen in a private house," Monsieur Arseneault said as he led Ginger and Felicia past a family dining area and down the stairs to the basement. This led them into a large, bright kitchen with a window looking out onto the red-brick wall of an area that was open at the top to the street to let in sunlight. "But I want complete privacy and isolation when I am inventing. I have no interest in running a restaurant right now and I rely heavily on my wife at my side to taste my new creations."

The first thing Ginger noticed were the many hanging racks containing dozens of copper pots and pans of varying sizes. Along the walls there were long wooden doorless cupboards with more ceramic and copper-bottomed cookware. Kitchen utensils, such as large stirring spoons and knives, were also hanging on racks along the walls. Most prominent was a large and very modern-looking, smooth-topped, gas-fired combination oven and range with modern heat regulators and two-tone finish. The floor was black and white tile that was set off by the brown and red brick walls and cream-coloured ceiling.

The kitchen rivalled the size of some small hotel kitchens, and Ginger couldn't recall ever being in a more modern one. The room was spotless, but Ginger could detect a faint smell of *herbes de Provence,* a smell she was familiar with from dining in many French homes, especially during the war. This version must have had a good portion of lavender, judging by the fragrance.

"I designed zees kitchen myself and it's almost sree times zee size of zee original kitchen. It has all zee latest features. The stove itself is a marvel and quite rare, even in London."

"Very impressive," Ginger said with genuine admiration.

"At zee moment I have been working on a new version of *cassoulet* using duck. I sink I have discovered a beautiful combination of white wine, leeks, and garlic zat is *magnifique…*" He kissed his fingertips and then waved his hand in the typical French fashion. "And when zee duck is properly prepared using goose fat instead of olive oil, and zen paired with zee right cheese—" He paused for a moment. "Forgive me, I am sure you deed not come here for a cookery lesson."

"So I imagine that while you are cooking and trying out new combinations, you are making notes in a book," Ginger said.

"Yes, zat is correct. And when I am done, I put zee notebook in my safe. I will deliver zee recipes to zee publisher, only when I feel I have enough of zem to make zee book."

"How about if you leave the kitchen for a moment, perhaps to have a break?" Ginger glanced about, taking in the nearest door that led to the passage. A thief was unlikely to escape through the window.

The chef shrugged. "I suppose zere have been short periods of time when zee book is left here unattended. But never more zan a few moments, and I simply cannot imagine my wife coming in here with nefarious intentions, or even my son for zat matter."

Ginger knew from experience that just because something was unimaginable did not mean it was impossible.

"Of course, you are probably right," Ginger said. "Is it possible to see the safe?"

Monsieur Arseneault led them to an adjacent room which served as an office with an oak desk and leather chair. There was a small combination safe sitting on top of a wooden table in the corner. Ginger noted there was no lock on the office door and the safe was not hidden or secured to the room in any way. Glancing out of the window, Ginger saw that it opened to a red-bricked window well. Even though it was accessed by the private courtyard at the back of the house, a thief with some skills could indeed gain access to the back garden and through this window if it was unlocked or open. The safe itself did not seem too much of an obstacle for a practiced safecracker. The notebook had not actually been stolen, however. Ginger guessed that if Monsieur Arseneault was correct and his recipes had actually been taken, the thief had instead used a camera to photograph the pages and later transcribed them. This made climbing in and out of the window well a little bit more challenging if one had a camera and even perhaps a tripod in tow, though it could explain why Monsieur Arseneault had not realised anyone had seen his notebook until much later.

Monsieur Arseneault approached the safe and turned the tumbler several times anti-clockwise and then once clockwise. There was a soft clicking sound and the door swung open. He reached in, took out a leather-bound notebook, and solemnly handed it to Ginger.

"Madame," he said simply. Ginger carefully opened the notebook and leafed through the pages, each one containing meticulously handwritten instructions and lists, all in French. She noticed one was titled *Ratatouille*. Felicia leaned close also, to get a glimpse. After a moment more, Ginger closed the book and handed it back to Monsieur Arseneault, who then placed it back in the safe.

"Thank you, Monsieur Arseneault. I realise that not many people have the privilege of seeing that book. Now, do you recall anyone coming into your home at any time in the last few months carrying a camera?" Ginger asked

The chef thought for a moment. "Yes, a few months ago zere was a day organised by my publisher to welcome zee members of zee press. Zese men were from newspapers, or food critics for magazines. Many of zem had cameras. Zey arrived at ten o'clock and were finished by eleven. But I promise you, my notebook was in my safe zee whole time."

On their way back to the kitchen, Ginger said, "You mentioned a maid earlier."

"Yes, zat is correct. We have a part-time maid. A very capable young woman. Her name is Brigitte and she comes in every day for three hours to clean and has done so for nearly five years. She never, never comes into zee kitchen when I am cooking, although she does clean up afterwards. Of course she was zee first person we sought of and I suppose it ees possible she could have sneaked in here while I was taking a short break. She denies it, of course."

Ginger asked Felicia to make note of the maid's name. The only motive Ginger could conceive of was money. Would the chefs involved have used the recipes if they'd known they were stolen? Perhaps, out of spite. Would one of them have paid for the privilege? Anything was possible.

"Thank you for your time, Monsieur Arseneault," Ginger said. "I think we have everything we need for now."

Ginger found Boss engaged in a game of tug-of-war with François, an old piece of thick rope tied into a knot being the coveted item. François seemed to be coming out ahead in the contest due to his significant girth, but Boss remained attached to the toy despite being dragged across the floor, growling and straining. The affair was immensely amusing and Ginger couldn't help but laugh. François let out one of his frequent sneezes thereby suddenly letting go of the toy, sending Boss sprawling. Mme Arseneault clapped with delight.

"Feel free to bring Boss around anytime," Mme Arseneault said as Ginger and Felicia stepped out onto the street.

"That was an enjoyable visit," Felicia remarked as they returned to the motorcar. "And now I have the feeling you are intent on the next phase of our plan." She smiled at Ginger as the Crossley started moving forward. "I would imagine it involves visiting more kitchens."

"Yes," Ginger agreed. "It seems that there are perhaps a few unscrupulous chefs in our fair city, and I am curious to hear how creative they will be at denying it."

*G*inger drove the Crossley through Kensington Gardens at her usual frightening speed, which Felicia found terrifying, and Boss thrilling.

"Really, Ginger," Felicia snapped. "You almost hit that cart!"

"Nonsense," Ginger said with a flick of her gloved hand. "There was plenty of room."

"The lad jumped out of the way to save his life!"

"Like I said, there was plenty of room."

As they entered Soho, thoughts about the visit to the Arseneaults' house ran through Ginger's head. Monsieur Arseneault was indeed an enigmatic figure. On the one hand, he was rather arrogant and opinionated, but on the other he was a brilliant chef. Ginger imagined he could be hard to live or work with, though it appeared that the Arseneaults had enjoyed a long and seemingly successful marriage. Ginger's first marriage had been cut short by tragedy and her second had only just begun. When she observed couples who had been together for decades she sometimes became wistful, wondering what that must be like. Ginger found Madame Arseneault to be a beautiful, kind, and open-hearted lady who seemed to be quite content. This meant certainly that Monsieur Arseneault possessed endearing qualities that were not apparent at first blush. Ginger wondered about the couple's history, where they had met, and how the romance had first started—clearly sometime long before the war.

The first three chefs they visited that afternoon were very uncooperative and dismissive. Ginger grew increasingly frustrated, coming to the end of her patience with rude chefs who regarded two female investigators as beneath them. She couldn't help but wonder if she and Felicia were indeed on a wild goose chase.

The fourth chef, a stout middle-aged man named Mr. Arthur who owned a restaurant on Marshall Street called The Bristol, was also defiant at first when they questioned him alone in his office.

"Mr. Arthur, your restaurant is known for English cuisine and yet you have one conspicuous dish that, according to your head waiter whom we have just questioned, has been recently added."

The chef snorted. "What of it?"

"It is a French dish, Mr. Arthur, from the south-east of France I believe, called *pieds paquets* or stewed lambs' feet. Your head waiter says it has been a huge success and that you plan on expanding your cuisine based on the success of this one item. Are you trained in French cookery, Mr. Arthur?"

"I have some training," he said defensively. "In fact I was quite good at French cookery when I was younger... Well, that *was* a long time ago."

"Where did you get this recipe?"

Mr. Arthur's bulbous eyes blinked rapidly, and he refused to look Ginger in the eye.

"I urge you to tell me the truth," Ginger said. "You are a respected chef!"

"I have not broken any laws!" he said finally. "Yes... the recipe was given to me." He let out a long sigh, and then continued, "A young man walked into my restaurant kitchen a few weeks ago, and without introducing himself simply handed me the written recipe. He told me that this recipe was sure to be a big success to the point that it could revolutionise our cuisine here. That's all he said. Can you imagine such a thing?"

"Go on," Ginger said.

"He turned and walked away, simple as you please, without another word. You can imagine I was inclined to throw the thing away, but then I read the recipe…"

"…and?" Felicia asked.

"I knew right away this could not have come from such a young man. This was the work of a seasoned chef. The combination of ingredients for the sauce was unusual and bold. The recipe was very detailed to the point of the year and origin of the white wine used to cook it. Even the province the tomatoes for the sauce were to be grown in was specified. I knew immediately that either this dish would taste terrible or it would be a true masterpiece. It took me a while to gather the ingredients exactly to specification. Some of the food markets that carried these particular items were new to me. Then, when I was ready, I came in early one morning and cooked a single portion of the dish myself, not trusting any of my chefs with such a thing." The man took off his chef's hat and wiped his forehead, "My God, I felt like Mozart's *Salieri.* My own work paling in comparison to this divinely inspired triumph. I could never contrive such a *tour de force.* As soon as the food touched my tongue I was instantly jealous, may God forgive me. The dish tasted like something served in the very banqueting halls of heaven by blessed angels on winged feet!" The chef sat staring straight ahead as if he were at that moment having a vision.

Oh mercy. What a most unusual confession! There was no longer any doubt that Monsieur Arseneault was right; someone had indeed been stealing his recipes.

"Can you give me a description of the young man?" Ginger asked.

Mr. Arthur lifted a thick shoulder then said, "He was tall, decent enough looking, with a lanky frame and dark hair... a moustache, I think. He had a long, slender nose, but the most memorable feature was a prominent Adam's apple."

7

*H*ow serendipitous that Jean Claude Arseneault had invited Felicia to see him play at his club, the Lonely Street Cabaret.

"I have been in here before," Felicia said, "but it's been a while."

Ginger and Felicia stepped into the candle-lit, smoke-filled interior. The satin tangerine day dress with buttoned sleeves and a narrow, pleated, low-waisted skirt that Ginger wore was a little understated for the environment. She wasn't there to be entertained, and for business her outfit was perfectly suited.

The walls of the club were covered in gold-printed wallpaper, while the beams and doorframes were of rich, dark oak wood. The round, candle-lit tables were covered with white tablecloths, and surrounded by wicker chairs. It was still early evening, so the place was only about half full with clientele, the women all dressed in flapper-style outfits and the men in lounge suits, enjoying a drink or a cigarette over quiet conversation. Behind the bar was a huge assortment of whisky, brandy, vodka, and other spirits all placed on several large, mirrored shelves. A barman behind the counter prepared the drinks.

At the back of the room stood a wooden stage with an upright piano, a small three-piece drum set, and a double bass.

"Oh look," Ginger said as Jean Claude Arseneault, along with two young black musicians, came onto the stage from the left and took their places at the instruments. "It seems we have come just at the right moment."

Before long, the room was filled with soft, smooth music of the style that Ginger had heard being played occasionally on BBC radio. She also recognised it from her years living in Boston just before her return to London. The American music genre was becoming increasingly popular in London along with its livelier forms, and Ginger guessed that it was all part of the transatlantic exchange that was still happening in the wake of war.

The world had somehow become smaller in the last ten years, Ginger mused as she listened to the soft, swinging rhythms and beautiful, complicated melodies that the younger Mr. Arseneault seemed to play so effortlessly. Was it possible this talented young man carried such vindictiveness towards his father?

"He is rather smashing," Felicia said, gazing dreamily at the stage.

After ordering a Brandy Alexander for herself and a Grasshopper for Felicia, Ginger sat and quietly listened to the music. Her intention was to confront Jean Claude Arseneault, perhaps during one of the music breaks, before she went to Monsieur Arseneault with the sad news that his own son was against him.

Ginger made note of everyone in the room, and a particular young man sitting at a corner table nursing a drink caught her eye. He looked familiar, but it was difficult to clearly see his face due to the dim lighting and the fog of cigarette smoke hanging in the air.

"Isn't that Mr. Kendrick, Monsieur Arseneault's former student?"

Felicia turned to look. "Yes, I think it is."

"How interesting that he should turn up here," Ginger said. "He must be a friend of Mr. Arseneault's."

"He did spend a good deal of time at the Arseneaults' house," Felicia said, "and they're roughly the same age."

Felicia was right, thought Ginger. The two could have struck up a friendship, perhaps even based on mutual grievances against Monsieur Arseneault, if there were indeed such feelings on the part of Jean Claude for unknown reasons.

"Shall we?" Ginger said. Felicia nodded, and they picked up their drinks and headed towards Mr. Kendrick's table.

"May we join you?" Felicia asked. She and Ginger didn't wait for an answer as they slid into the chairs opposite William Kendrick.

"Oh, this is just dashed awkward, isn't it? You two again." Mr. Kendrick's slurred speech and red eyes confirmed that he was already deeply in his cups.

Felicia shared a look with Ginger, then pressed on. "So, fancy meeting you here, Mr. Kendrick. Are you a friend of Monsieur Arseneault's son?"

"Which one?" Mr. Kendrick let out a sardonic chuckle. "It's bloody hard to tell them apart sometimes."

Ginger and Felicia shared another look. How drunk was he?

"Blimey." Mr. Kendrick's smile disappeared and he stared at them with a wild look in his pickled eyes, as if he had let something important slip. "I'm not talking to you two anymore!" He lifted his glass to his mouth.

Ginger suddenly remembered what Mr. Kendrick's landlord had said about a young Frenchman sharing a flat with him.

"Mr. Kendrick," Ginger began, "does Jean Claude have a brother?"

The man glared at them before sliding out of his seat and standing up shakily. He opened his mouth to say something more, but thought better of it and headed for the exit, shooting a glance across the room to the stage where the young Mr. Arseneault was focused on smooth jazz.

8

The next afternoon, Ginger and Felicia, with Boss in the backseat, drove around the corner onto East Road in Edgware. A police constable walked his beat, while another could be seen on horseback a distance down the road. Ginger had no idea if the French flatmate would be home, but she knew that Mr. Kendrick would be on his way to *The Guillotine*. There was no way of knowing what would happen when they spoke to the flatmate, so it was good to know there were police in the area.

The two-storey red-brick building was the last one on the cobblestoned street and Ginger parked in front of it. Large hedges acted as a visual barrier to the next street, giving the appearance of isolation. Ginger put Boss on a leash, then with Felicia entered the main entrance, which opened to a common concrete passageway.

They passed the landlord's flat, from which they could hear recorded music playing loudly.

"*Ethel Waters... 'I Found a New Baby',*" said Felicia, bobbing her head and moving her shoulders slightly to the beat. "I love this song."

Ginger smiled at the sight of her flapper sister-in-law. "This is no time for the foxtrot," she teased.

Ginger knocked on Mr. Kendrick's door, and when she received no answer, they just stood in the dingy corridor considering what to do next. From inside the flat they heard a very soft 'meow'.

"It's a cat," Ginger said. "Hmm, it sounds like it's in deep distress, don't you think?"

Felicia blinked once, then caught her meaning. "Oh, yes, it sounds like it's at death's door. Obviously half-starved and lying on the floor, close to breathing its last."

"I think someone may need to rescue it." Ginger tried the doorknob—it was unlocked.

"You have no fear!" exclaimed Felicia in a loud whisper. She was, of course, totally unaware of Ginger's wartime activities working for the British Secret Service. This would not be the first time Ginger had covertly searched someone's home.

"This flat faces directly onto the street," Ginger said in a hushed voice. "You and Boss can sit in the Crossley. If you see someone walking up this street who resembles Jean Claude, just sound the horn with two blasts. That will be the signal. Just pretend you are waiting impatiently for a friend on the other side of the street when you do it."

"Boo," Felicia said. "Why do you get all the fun?"

Ginger raised a brow and Felicia wiggled her fingers. "Come along, Boss."

Ginger stepped into the flat and was met by a young tabby cat who meowed softly while brushing Ginger's legs and purring loudly. "There you are. Glad to see you are all right after all." Ginger reached down and stroked it lightly while glancing around the room. The flat had a tiny kitchen area with unwashed dishes in the sink and a coal-burning stove. An adjoining sitting area had a grimy window looking onto the road. A narrow passage led to one large bedroom with unmade single beds along opposite walls.

At the end of the passage was a closed door and coming closer, Ginger recognised the acidic smell of chemicals used in darkrooms to develop photographs. She opened the door and felt for a light switch. The room was instantly bathed in a red, muted light. A table had several photograph developing trays lying on it, and hanging above were six photographs fastened with wooden clips to a string that stretched from wall to wall like a washing line.

Ginger studied the photographs. Four of them were images of streets and buildings Ginger recognised as being in Soho. One was of Mr. Kendrick standing in front of this block of flats wearing his chef's hat and a big grin. The last one was a snap of a young man posing beside *The Bromley*. He was wearing a suit and holding a trilby hat in one hand. At first glance Ginger thought it was Jean Claude Arseneault, but then she noticed that the hair was cut in a different style and was of a much lighter shade. His eyes were also set slightly wider apart. It was a close match but not identical—it had to be the mysterious sibling.

Ginger returned to the sitting room, and focused in on a small wooden cabinet in the corner. Moving quickly, she opened the top drawer. Inside were numerous folders, each one marked with a label. The first read *"Recette"*.

Oh mercy.

Inside were about a dozen photographs of recipes, most certainly from Monsieur Arseneault's notebook; Ginger immediately recognised the meticulous handwriting. Several of the photographs had pieces of paper clipped to them. On the pages were what looked like handwritten English translations of the photographs they were attached to.

Ginger stilled when two short blasts of the Crossley's horn sounded.

Slipping the folder into her handbag, Ginger closed the drawer and moved towards the door. As she opened it, she was once again met with the sound of Ethel Waters reverberating through the common passage. Just as she stepped out of the door a young man walked into the main entrance. He stopped short and glared at Ginger.

"What is this?" he said menacingly, in a soft French accent. She recognised him immediately from the hanging photograph. He must have come through or around those hedges at the end of the street, which would explain why Felicia had not had time to warn her properly.

Ginger shut the door behind her and adjusted her handbag strap on her shoulder. Caught in the act.

"I heard your cat in great distress. I thought I would just take a look and see if it was all right." It was a reasonable excuse and would be hard to disprove should the man want to press charges against Ginger for unauthorised entry.

The fellow stepped towards her with a questioning look on his face.

"Who are you? What do you want?" He was obviously a bit confused by Ginger's outfit and appearance. She certainly did not look like a burglar. Ginger moved to go around him and out of the door but he blocked her path.

"Not so fast," he said, his eyes narrowing. The jaunty music playing in the background provided a strange backdrop to the scene as Ginger considered employing one of the many self-defence manoeuvres she had been trained in during the war. A well-placed kick to the knee would do it. She shifted her weight and started to lift the hem of her dress slightly with her free right hand.

Just then, the entrance door opened and Felicia and Boss stepped in. The man didn't turn around, but kept his gaze on Ginger. Felicia's hand flew to her mouth in shock.

Boss let out a growl, shot forward, and grabbed the man's right trouser leg between his teeth, holding on tightly.

"*Mon Dieu!*" The fellow yelled as he hopped on one leg, unable to shake Boss loose.

"Or… that will do just as well," Ginger muttered. She

deftly stepped around her aggressor, grabbed Felicia by the arm, and ran for the door.

"Come, Boss!"

Boss took one final big tug, which threw the man off balance and made him drop to one knee with a shout, then scurried out of the door after Ginger.

Ginger scooped up the little dog, tossed him into the Crossley, jumped in, and hit the starter, skidding away from the kerb before Felicia had even finished slamming her door. The man rushed out of the door of the building, ran a few futile steps after the accelerating car, and then tore his newsboy cap from his head in frustration.

"Hey!" he yelled as they drove off.

When they had turned onto the next street, Ginger accelerated the motorcar to her normal breakneck speed, and Felicia let out a whoop as she held on to her hat.

9

"*H*is Christian name ees Pierre, he ees twenty-six years old, and his last name ees Bellerose—hees mother's, of course." Marcel Arseneault sat with his head in his hands, slumped forward in a chair facing Ginger's desk at the office of Lady Gold Investigations. The photographs and handwritten papers lay spread out in front of them.

"Yes," Monsieur Arseneault continued. "I knew I had another son, but I had no idea he was in London. I thought he was still in Paris." The weary-looking chef stared ahead blankly. "Flora ees also aware of Pierre, but Jean Claude ees not. I told her about heem many years ago. My wife ees a good woman." He swiped at a tear that trickled down his ruddy cheek. "She has forgiven me many times over zee last many years. I know zees may be hard for you to believe, but I can be sometimes temperamental, maybe even hard to live with at times."

Ginger glanced at Felicia who sat behind their client. Felicia's eyes widened and her lips pulled together as if that could keep at bay the grin that threatened to break out. Ginger had to look away before she too succumbed to inappropriate laughter.

Monsieur Arseneault continued, "Flora has always had a calming effect on me." He let out a long sigh. "I met Pierre's mother in Lyon when I was just finishing my training as a chef. I was on a break with some friends, and I met Adèle in a club one night. It was a short and troubled liaison and I ended it. A few months later, I met Flora, we started a beautiful relationship, and were married soon after. We were husband and wife for sree years already when I received a letter and a photograph from Lyon. Flora was at zat time carrying Jean Claude in her womb, and I was starting to gain some *renom* in Paris as a chef. Naturally, I was aghast."

He looked at Ginger with tearful eyes. "Zees little boy was obviously mine, judging from zees photograph. Anyway, zee letter contained a demand for money to help raise zee little boy. Flora believed zat we should send some money. Unfortunately eet did not end zere."

"She kept demanding money?" Ginger asked.

"Yes, we sent money a few more times, but zee demands kept getting larger. We finally stopped about a year later. I did not hear from her again and I don't know if she ees even still alive. I thought zees was zee end of zee whole affair. But a few years ago, we started getting letters from Pierre along with more photographs. He was now a grown man and entering photography as a career. He did not even mention his mother. I refused to send anything. I have a brother in Lyon named Antoine who ees a photograper for many years and he knew I had an illegitimate son, but deed not know any details. I asked heem if he knew any young photographers with zee first name Pierre who had a certain family resemblance. He did not, and he grew suspicious so he went to zee police. It seems Pierre ees a fugitive and a professional thief. Zee police believed zat he had fled to Paris."

"Obviously he has made his way to London," Ginger said. "He must have tracked you here and somehow befriended

William Kendrick. Probably after you fired him. The two collaborated on a revenge plot; however, that is a matter for the police. But these pictures are proof that the man did steal from you. I have already contacted my husband at Scotland Yard and he arrested Pierre Bellerose early this morning. There should be no problem convicting him. You can also expect the chief inspector to contact you. When a chief inspector from Scotland Yard accompanies you to certain restaurants, I am sure they will agree to immediately take your creations off their menus lest they face criminal charges."

"But how deed he do eet?" Monsieur Arseneault leaned forward in his chair and held his palms open.

"I believe it was a simple matter for him to pose as a member of the press on the day your publisher invited them all to your home," Ginger said. "I imagine that while most of the press was gathered around your new stove, which is one of the only models of its kind in London and surely would make an interesting entry into the story, Mr. Bellerose slipped into your office. I stood in your kitchen and estimated how this could be done. The entrance to the passage leading to your office is obscured by a large cupboard. Furthermore, your office is often left unlocked. Mr. Bellerose probably knew all of this from information given to him by Mr. Kendrick."

"*Incroyable!*"

"To a professional thief of any experience with combination locks, your safe would merely be an inconvenience," Ginger said. "I am sure he was able to crack it within a few minutes. From there it would simply be a matter of taking some pictures, the sound of which blended with the other clicking cameras and conversations taking place in the kitchen."

Monsieur Arseneault sat staring at Ginger as if trying to comprehend what he was hearing. "How can zees young man have such an agenda against me? I did him no harm at all. I suppose now I should reveal to Jean Claude zat he has a brother, but under zee circumstances it will not be a task I will enjoy."

"As far as motive goes, revenge for perceived injustice can be a strong motivator, even if it is misplaced," Ginger said, though she wasn't in full agreement that Pierre was without reason to feel abandoned by his father. "As far as Jean Claude is concerned, he may already know he has a brother. We did find Mr. Kendrick at the club where your son Jean Claude plays. It's possible that he may have introduced Pierre to him."

Monsieur Arseneault slumped back in his chair with his hand on his forehead. "I sink I have a headache." He closed his eyes for a moment shaking his head, "Zat ungrateful Kendrick."

"We actually don't have any evidence that Mr. Kendrick himself was involved in the actual crime of stealing these recipes, although he may certainly be complicit," Ginger said. "That is something for the police to investigate if they choose to in light of the evidence we have uncovered."

Monsieur Arseneault sighed again and then sat up straight. "You and your husband, along with you, Miss Gold, must come and dine with me and my wife in our home. I am deeply grateful for your diligence in zees matter. I will cook zee best *Boeuf Bourguignon* zat you have ever known. Eet will have no equal in all of England."

"It would be our pleasure," Ginger said sincerely.

"And you must bring your dog." The chef pointed at Boss who, knowing the word "dog", sat up and furiously started wagging his stump.

"François would be grateful for zee company," the chef continued. "My wife ees still talking about how much she enjoyed having Boss come to visit her fat little dog." He looked steadily at Felicia. "I am sure Jean Claude would enjoy seeing you again, miss."

Felicia blinked twice and smiled demurely. "That sounds like the bee's knees."

THE CASE OF THE
MUSEUM BURGLARY

1

*G*inger tipped back her head to look up at the tall red-brick façade of the Wainwright Museum of Persia, housed in the former Wainwright Manor in Ilford, East London. For her evening visit to the museum, Ginger had chosen to wear an emerald-green linen coat with wide cuffs on the long sleeves, and a broad collar fastened with one of two oversized matching buttons, the second appearing at the hip. As she approached the huge oak doors that served as the main entrance, she tucked Boss, her small black and white Boston terrier, more securely under her arm. She'd meant to leave him in the Crossley, but at the last minute swooped him up, having been unnerved by a group of street urchins who'd materialized suddenly.

Felicia, who was Ginger's sister-in-law from her first marriage and her dear friend besides, followed closely.

"I've only agreed to come because Grandmama is insisting I become more cultured," Felicia remarked. "She doesn't accept that modern art and music is culture too."

Ginger smiled inwardly. She was quite fond of the strong-headed matriarch known in society as the Dowager Lady

Gold, but she knew also from experience that Ambrosia was indeed a force to contend with.

Having been invited by the museum's curator, Mr. William Hammond, Ginger and Felicia arrived specifically for a special "pre-opening" viewing of an exhibition of ancient clothing. Mr. Hammond's wife, Florence, was a regular customer at Ginger's shop, Feathers & Flair, and she and Ginger had become good friends due to a common interest in fashion, no matter what era or country. Ginger was delighted and felt honoured to be allowed to see the exhibits before the general public. The newspapers had placed the museum's special event on the front pages and Ginger gathered that on opening day this building would be filled to capacity with London's upper class.

Mr. Hammond had told them to come in on Sunday evening when most of the workers who were busy with renovations of the third floor would not be there and the place would be relatively quiet, though there were still a few caretakers on site, busying themselves in the final cleaning of the plush carpeted floors and setting up signs.

"Good evening, Mr. Hammond!"

The head curator pivoted at the sound of Ginger's voice, and a broad smile under a thin moustache took over his long, slender face.

"Mrs. Reed, you came!"

"Of course," Ginger said, shaking the man's hand. "I said I would. And may I introduce Miss Gold, my sister-in-law?"

"How do you do?" Mr. Hammond said politely. His eyes, framed with worry lines, noticed Boss in Ginger's arms, and despite propriety, he failed to keep his lips, and thus his moustache, from pulling down.

"This is Boss," Ginger said. "I do apologise for bringing him along, an oversight on my part, but I do hope you'll give him a pass. He's very well behaved."

"I can vouch for him," Felicia said. She had the smooth

porcelain skin of youth, an attractive mouth, and thick eyelashes that she now batted shamelessly.

Ginger would have been abashed if she weren't amused.

Mr. Hammond wasn't immune to Felicia's charms. "In—indeed," he stammered, then with a long inhale, as if to fortify himself, he took charge.

"On the ground floor, as you can see, we've featured weaponry, fishing equipment, and pottery from the era of the Safavid Dynasty, who ruled the Persian Empire in the sixteenth and seventeenth centuries. We thought it particularly fitting to house the exhibition here, as this building dates from 1622. Up the stairs, on the first floor, is where you will find the new exhibition displaying the clothing. My wife informed me that that is your area of interest."

"Indeed, it is," Ginger said. "Do you mind if we head upstairs?"

"Not at all. If you need anything, let me know. I've got a small task to attend to, and I'll return shortly."

Plush green carpet ran up a wide wooden staircase, and as they turned the corner to the first floor, Ginger gasped in delight. The entire floor was like a dress shop from ancient times.

"Such exciting ideas they had," Felicia said after studying the first glass-encased display which showed some examples of ornate outer garments that were worn by both men and women of the early part of the dynasty in the 1500s. The clothing was either placed on mannequins or laid flat with informational labels beneath each article. Ginger was fascinated to discover that clothing during that part of the Persian Empire was not marked primarily by gender, but also by social status or class. Men and women sometimes wore very similar outer garments and both used makeup.

Ginger placed Boss on the floor. "Stay by my side, Bossy." The little dog proved his intelligence by doing just that, walking and stopping in tandem with Ginger. She moved on to a display that featured ornately decorated trousers embroidered with rich colours of lapis blue, emerald green, and bright tomato red.

"So interesting," Ginger said, as she unfastened the two buttons of her jacket. She was feeling rather warm now that she'd been inside for some time. "The fabrics became more detailed and elaborate as the dynasty grew in size and wealth. Look at these amazing colours. They must have used some very exotic dyes for these materials."

Ginger and Felicia slowly made their way through the different exhibits, stopping often to read the panels fastened below the glass, which were filled with interesting facts to educate the museum visitors. Ginger and Felicia subconsciously kept their conversation at a low volume, even though they were alone—the general effect of the place was similar to that of a large library.

Suddenly, the lights flickered and then went out, plunging the entire museum into complete darkness. Boss let out a single bark.

"What on earth?" Felicia said

Ginger's war-era instincts kicked in. In her mind she mapped out exactly where she stood in relation to the exit, creating a mental map of each exhibit. "It's best just to stand still for the moment," she said calmly to Felicia, who stood about ten feet away to her right. Ginger continued, "We don't want to trip over something or break a valuable artefact. It's probably just a failure in the electrical room; I am sure they will have it back working in a moment."

Before long, the light from a hand-held torch could be seen coming up the stairs and a man's voice said, "It's all right. Someone has gone down to the cellars to check on the wires. We should be up and running in…"

At that moment, the lights flickered on and both Ginger and Felicia sighed in relief.

A portly man in his early forties with sandy hair and

moustache turned off his torch. He forced a chuckle. "See there. Just like I said." He turned back down the steps without another word.

Felicia looked at Ginger and shrugged. "Grandmama might be right about the value of oil lamps."

Ginger leaned down to give Boss a pat on the head, but her dog was nowhere in sight.

"Boss?"

Ginger and Felicia started slowly walking around the room looking behind the exhibits. "Well, this is certainly very odd. He never runs off like this," Ginger said. She called out again. "Boss?"

After searching the first floor, they quickly took the stairs down to the ground level to continue looking. A hot thread of worry twisted in Ginger's chest.

"Mrs. Reed?" Mr. Hammond had reappeared. "Is there something I can help you with?"

Ginger cast a sheepish look at him. After boasting about Boss' good behaviour, she now had to confess that he'd run off.

"I'm afraid my dog was frightened when the lights went out."

Mr. Hammond's mouth tightened and his eyes narrowed with disapproval.

"It's really not like him to do such a thing," Ginger explained. "He never runs off like that. He is a very well-trained dog."

"Indeed. Well, the doors to the street are closed. He can't have gone far."

Just then, they heard three short barks that sounded as if they came from the floor below.

"It appears that your pet has run down into the cellar," Mr. Hammond said. He snorted softly, then headed down a corridor to a door which was open just wide enough for a small dog to squeeze through. He opened it all the way, and then headed down a steep set of stairs.

"Watch your step," he said over his shoulder as Ginger and Felicia followed.

At the bottom of the steps there was a wall with the corridor leading off to the left and right.

Ginger called, "Boss?"

Two small barks came from their right. Ginger rushed down the wide corridor. Boss was sniffing under a small table that stood at the end of the corridor. There was a small hole in the wall at floor level.

"Mice?" said Ginger, feeling a hint of disbelief. "I thought we had talked about this before, Bossy."

To Mr. Hammond, who looked duly unimpressed, she added, "We have a slight rodent problem at Hartigan House. It's immensely amusing to Boss."

To Ginger's left was a large steel door locked with a padlock. Boss suddenly stopped sniffing at the hole and stared intently at the steel door. He sat perfectly still, his ears perked forward.

Mr. Hammond answered the unspoken question in the air. "This is the vault room. It holds all the artefacts not ready for display." His eyebrows were furrowed together as he stared at the large padlock thoughtfully. After a moment he finally took out a set of keys, opened the door, and turned on the light. The dusty-smelling red-brick room was filled with several rows of cloth-covered boxes and crates. Numbers and letters were written on signs above each section to identify them. Boss ran in and jumped up on one of the lower boxes. A loud gasp came from Mr. Hammond.

"I'm so sorry, Mr. Hammond," Ginger said. "I really don't know what's got into him. Boss! Come here this instant!"

Boss promptly obeyed and Ginger hoped her embarrassment had finally come to an end.

But Mr. Hammond seemed no longer interested in Boss'

foibles. He was staring at a small, rectangular walnut box adjacent to the crate Boss had jumped on. "My God!" he muttered. The box in question was wide open. "It's gone! It should be right in here." He faced Ginger and Felicia with eyes filled with panic.

"What is it?" Ginger asked, stepping closer.

"We've been robbed."

All three sets of eyes landed on Boss as he blinked up at them, looking quite pleased with himself.

2

"My wife tells me you are a private detective," Mr. Hammond said with a shaky voice, after he had sat down in his office. The room was spacious and tastefully decorated, with two windows overlooking the manor grounds. In addition to Mr. Hammond's large oak desk and leather chair, there were two rich leather wingback chairs and a sizeable sofa.

Yes, I am," Ginger said as she and Felicia claimed seats. Ginger removed her coat, revealing an ivory day blouse matched with a pleated skirt. "But, Mr. Hammond, don't you want to call the police?"

Mr. Hammond shook his head. "Not just yet, for reasons I will explain in a moment." The poor man looked very distraught indeed and Ginger's investigative curiosity was definitely piqued.

He locked his gaze with hers. "Will you help me?"

Ginger didn't think it wise to keep the police out of it, but for the sake of her friendship with Mrs. Hammond she found herself agreeing. "The first thing you need to do is lock the outside doors to keep anyone from coming or going. Then we need to gather everyone; all the attendants, workers, and custodians together in one room. Make sure they are all accounted for. This must be done immediately if we want to catch this thief."

Mr. Hammond quickly nodded, rose from his chair and walked to the door and called out across the hall. "Mr. Steadman!"

A fair-skinned man with blond hair turning to grey appeared. Ginger recognised him as the man who had arrived as a saviour with a torch earlier.

"Mr. Steadman, please lock all the doors and gather the staff in the upper lounge area immediately."

"What's going on, Mr. Hammond?"

"I will explain everything in the lounge. Please hurry."

Mr. Hammond returned to his seat. "That was Mr. Steadman, the second curator."

"I see," Ginger paused for a moment, then asked, "What is the object that has been stolen?"

Mr. Hammond swallowed hard. "It's a very valuable artefact, and it was scheduled for the Persian Jewellery exhibition which is set to open in three weeks' time on the manor's top floor. Renovations to that level are not quite done yet so all the jewellery is being stored in our cellar which I thought would be very secure."

"Was there anything else stolen?"

"Not that I can tell, but a lot of the other jewellery is actually not that valuable in the grand scheme of things. The thief obviously knew exactly where to look within the vault for this object."

"How did you know someone had been in the vault?"

"The padlock was turned backwards. The keyhole was facing the door. That means you have to reach down with your left hand to turn it while you put the key in with the other." Mr. Hammond looked intently at the two ladies as if this explained everything.

"I see," Ginger said.

"This takes more effort and is less efficient. I have got into the habit of always leaving the keyhole pointing outwards. I have been doing it that way every day for years. That's how I knew someone had tampered with it. Even Mr. Steadman has been instructed not to go inside the vault without my being present except in case of extreme emergency."

"Who else has a key to that padlock?" Ginger asked

"Just me and Mr. Steadman. We are also the only ones with keys to the building and the only two people who know what the contents of the vault are."

"How do you know no one else knows the contents of the vault? There must be a list?" Ginger asked.

"Yes, there is. I have it here in the bottom drawer of my desk." He reached down and pulled out a large wooden clipboard and handed it to Ginger. There was a long list of numbered items typed on paper. Number thirty-four was listed as a 'Jewelled Persian Dagger'. "I didn't think to lock it up," he said thoughtfully. "I suppose someone could have come in here and taken a look if they were determined to find it. Oh dear, do you think that was my undoing?"

"That is unknown right now I'm afraid, but very likely yes," Ginger said as she handed the clipboard back. Mr. Hammond's shoulders sagged as he let out a long sigh.

"Do you know where Mr. Steadman was when the lights went out?"

"Yes, we were both in here having a brandy," said Mr. Hammond. "When the lights went out we each took one of the hand-held torches that I keep here behind me in this cabinet. I went down to check on the fuse room while Steadman went to calm everyone and make sure nothing was accidentally broken in the dark. There is some very valuable pottery on display."

Boss jumped onto Ginger's lap and she scratched him behind the ears. "And what did you find in the fuse room?"

"Both of the main glass fuses were slightly loose. Although that was odd, it wasn't unreasonable to imagine they could have gradually come loose over time. There were some road works done in the area here a few weeks ago. That could have made all the nearby buildings shake slightly, I imagine. Anyway, it took me only a moment to screw them back in. Then, after the lights came on, I immediately came back to the office and Steadman was already here to meet me. After that he went back to work." His eyes landed on Boss, his gaze softer now. "A few moments later I heard you calling out for your dog."

"Is there a back way out of the cellar level?"

"Currently the only way out of the building is up and through this level at the front door. The cellar doors are locked and I have the only key but yes, the fuse room is on the other side of the manor and so it has a separate stairway leading up to this floor as well as a hallway connecting it to the vault area."

"So in other words," Ginger said, "the thief could have gone down and loosened the fuses, then, armed with a torch, gone directly to the vault to somehow open it, steal the artefact, and then make his way up to this level again without passing you as you went to check the fuses."

"Yes," said Mr. Hammond thoughtfully. "I suppose that is correct. But I would have noticed if someone had gone all the way to the front entrance to leave the building just then. Those doors are solid oak and twelve feet high, and when they open, they create a large draught throughout the building. They are also very noisy as the hinges still haven't been oiled properly."

Ginger and Felicia had noticed that when they'd entered the building.

"When did you last see the stolen object?"

"I checked on it and all the other pieces at eight o'clock, shortly before the lights went out."

Ginger hummed. "That means the object is almost certainly still in the building and so is the perpetrator."

Mr. Hammond's face went white.

"I am assuming you have a night watchman here when the museum is closed?" Ginger asked.

"Yes, we have two guards here hired from a reputable firm that specialises in protecting museums from robbery."

"That explains why the thief chose to come during the day," Felicia remarked.

"How many people are working here this evening?" asked Ginger.

Mr. Hammond thought for a moment. "Five people including Steadman, myself, and Miss Greene, my private secretary. Does this mean you are taking the case? I don't mind paying your fee."

"The fee is the least of your worries, I think," Ginger said, "but I suppose I don't have a choice at this point if we really want to catch this thief. But keep in mind, I can't hold everyone here hostage for very long just on my own authority. If we let them all go however, the robber could be long gone by the time the police can get here."

Mr. Hammond sighed, leaned back in his chair, pulled out his handkerchief and dabbed at his damp forehead.

"Now," said Ginger, "Please tell me more about this arte-fact and why you don't wish to inform the police."

3

"*I*t is called 'The Blade of T'Abriz', a ceremonial dagger that was made for and worn by the Shah of Azerbaijan in the early 1500s. It is very rare because the blade is made from Persian black Damascus steel. It was more for decoration than for any practical use. It is encased in a red velvet-covered wooden sheath with gilt floral embroidery and black and white piping."

Mr. Hammond showed them a picture of a small dagger with an ornately decorated hilt with two large, dark-coloured precious stones which were framed with many smaller diamonds. In the picture the velvet sheath was lying beside it on a black background.

"This is a recent photograph. These stones are sapphires; the hilt is gold. The Shah died in 1524 after which the dagger's history is somewhat unclear, but eventually, in 1856 it somehow ended up in the hands of a group of private art collectors and their families. These art collectors are based in Egypt and they are simply known as *Aljamaeia* or 'The Collective'. They are somewhat mysterious but extremely influential in the world of antiquities. It is this group that has started and now funds this private museum. They have eight more museums in England and four in Egypt, with several more smaller exhibitions scattered throughout Europe."

"Impressive," Ginger remarked. She dearly wanted to rescue this amazing artefact, if only to see it for herself.

Felicia was apparently impressed by other factors. "How much is the Blade of T'Abriz worth?"

"It's incredibly difficult to ascribe worth to such a thing," Mr. Hammond said, "because artefacts like this are irreplaceable. But, as you know, there has been a recent rise in interest in all things old and bejewelled due to the discovery of King Tut's tomb a few years ago. Currently, the dagger is valued at approximately five thousand pounds sterling."

Felicia blew air out of her cheeks and fell back in her chair.

Ginger stared intently at Mr. Hammond. "What is your connection with this Collective?"

"Well, that's just it, you see," Mr. Hammond started. "Being a curator of a museum like this has been a lifelong dream for me. It took me over two years to convince them to consider this museum and to employ me in this job. I had to travel to Egypt six times to meet the various parties involved. It's a highly competitive field and my hope is to eventually be considered for the position of head curator for one of their larger museums."

Mr. Hammond paused and looked at both women. "The Blade of T'Abriz was given to this museum with reluctance. It is one of The Collective's more prized artefacts. If news got out that it had been stolen under my care, not only would my career be over but it would make international headlines. They might even shut down this museum as well. No one has ever stolen from *Aljamaeia* before." Another pause. "So you see my dilemma."

"Certainly, Mr. Hammond," said Ginger carefully. "Now, you may not be aware of this, but my husband is Chief Inspector Basil Reed of Scotland Yard."

Mr. Hammond's eyes grew wide. "Oh?"

Ginger went on. "He is normally involved in murder cases, but I really think at this point it is necessary to involve him at least in a limited way. I can ask him to make sure it doesn't go to the press. I'm not certain where this will all lead but it might be good to have the resources of Scotland Yard on our side for a theft of this magnitude. For example, they have a record of known criminals in the country. That fact alone is worth engaging my husband. There may also be insurance issues if we don't report this to the police, not to mention the fact that should we not solve this crime, and The Collective finds out you did not immediately go to the police—"

Mr. Hammond interrupted, "I thought of that too, Mrs. Reed. But can we contain all of this in a discreet manner? In what way do you want to involve your husband?"

"I will give him a list of the names of your staff, first of all," said Ginger. "Then I want to ask if he can send two or three constables to guard the outside perimeter of the museum. That will ensure that the place is sealed and will increase our chances considerably. They can be dressed in plain clothes so as not to attract attention."

"I suppose you are right," Mr. Hammond conceded. He went to a filing cabinet and pulled out a piece of paper. "This is a list of the names of all the people who work here. Twelve in all. I will mark the people who are here today, five including myself." He put a tick beside some names on the list.

"May I please use your telephone?" asked Ginger. "It's Sunday evening so Basil will be at home right now but he can ring the office at Scotland Yard." Mr. Hammond motioned to the older-style candlestick contraption on his desk.

After Ginger had described the events of the evening to Basil, he agreed that he could keep the matter away from the press. In addition, he said he would personally check on the list of names and send over two constables in plain clothes so as not to attract attention.

"They should be there soon but they won't come in until you tell them to or until something happens to warrant them entering the building," he said. "It sounds like there might be an arrest made tonight, so you'll definitely need them there at some point. Be careful, love. There's no telling what a desperate thief is capable of."

Ginger hung the cone-shaped earpiece on the stand and turned to Mr. Hammond. "Now just a question or two more before we interview the workers here. Were you in charge of choosing them all?"

"My secretary, Miss Greene, helped me with the interviews. Each applicant came with impeccable credentials."

"And how long has Miss Greene been with you?" asked Ginger.

"It must be six months now. She had already worked for a reputable museum in Wales, so she too came with good credentials."

"After we interview everyone, we are going to have to make a preliminary search of the place, Mr. Hammond. I wish we could do that first but at this point everyone here is a suspect. Since it's unlikely that the thief has already fled, time is of the essence. We'll do the search in groups to make it go faster and we will ourselves specify who are in those groups. This will ensure that the thief, or thieves, cannot give a false report."

"I understand," Mr. Hammond said. "Fortunately, this is not a very large place so it shouldn't take too long to search."

"All right then." Ginger placed Boss on the floor, then stood. "Let's get on with this, shall we?"

4

$\mathcal{L}$ ike the rest of the building, the first-floor lounge area was lavishly decorated with thick carpet and comfortable furniture. Two sofas and six plush wing back chairs were placed in a large square around a beautiful low wooden serving table. The tall windows in this particular room had not been darkened, and allowed for a nice view of the rear grounds. The high, arched ceilings gave the room a very spacious ambience. A chandelier hung just above the serving table.

Four men, including Mr. Hammond and Mr. Steadman, sat opposite each other on the sofas. Two of them wore custodians' uniforms. A young woman dressed in a frock of purple crepe satin with stylish bell pleats sat in one of the chairs adjacent to Mr. Steadman.

Since some of the staff had not yet met Ginger and Felicia, Mr. Hammond made all the introductions, and then cleared his throat. "I am so sorry to have to lock all the doors and to request this meeting, but I'm afraid I have to ask that no one leave the building for the moment."

"Well, we are eager to hear what this is all about, sir," said a man Mr. Hammond had introduced as John Barnes. The chief caretaker had a slim, wiry appearance as if he were made of pipe cleaners.

Mr. Hammond responded grimly, "I am sorry to say that it looks like we have been robbed."

A round of gasping was followed by narrow glances towards their neighbours.

"That seems right impossible," a balding man protested.

"I'm afraid it's true, Mr. Billings," Mr. Hammond responded. "I've asked Mrs. Reed to help for now." He glanced Ginger's way nervously. "She's a renowned private detective."

A second round of gasping ensued.

"You mean t'say this 'appened when all o' the lights went out?" Mr. Billings spouted.

Mr. Hammond nodded heavily. "It seems so."

"What was it then?" Mr. Barnes asked. "The thing that was taken?"

Mr. Hammond looked to Ginger and sighed as if it pained him physically to admit the loss. "The missing object is a very valuable weapon known as the 'Blade of T'Abriz'. It is part of the collection for the new exhibition due to open soon on the third floor."

"That part of the building isn't even ready for the exhibition," added Miss Greene. "Wasn't it kept under lock and key?"

Mr. Hammond grunted. "Yes."

"But there are meant to be only two keys," Mr. Steadman said.

"Yes, Mr. Steadman," Ginger said, jumping in. "And you and Mr. Hammond are the caretakers of those keys. Mr. Hammond tells me you were in the office with him when the lights went out and that he was the one who went down the stairs."

Mr. Steadman leaned in. "That's where both the electrical room and the fuse box are located."

"Even though they are on different sides of the building?" Ginger said.

"That's correct," agreed Mr. Steadman.

"Are the police on the way?" asked Mr. Barnes.

"Not yet," Mr. Hammond said. "I'll explain why later."

Ginger had instructed Mr. Hammond to keep that part ambiguous. She realised that because of Boss' strange behaviour, the fact that the jewel was missing had been discovered far earlier than the thief had planned for. There was no telling how the robber would react to the news that the police were on their way and would soon be just outside the door.

"In the interest of privacy and safety," Ginger said, "we want to interview each of you separately in Mr. Hammond's office. The first will be Mr. Billings, please. The rest of you please stay here with Mr. Hammond."

Felicia and Ginger, with Boss in tow, headed with Mr. Billings down the steps to Mr. Hammond's office.

"Please empty your pockets, if you don't mind," Ginger said as she and Felicia sat down. "It's just a precaution."

Ginger pulled out her notebook and handed it to Felicia who opened it and started writing notes. Boss lay down on the plush carpet next to Ginger. They watched as Mr. Billings took off his cap and then dutifully emptied all his pockets onto the desk and then turned them inside out. There was some loose change, a small cleaning rag, a box of matches, and a packet of Player's Navy Cut cigarettes. Mr. Billings then sat down opposite the desk.

"Mr. Billings, can you tell us where you were when the lights went off?"

"I was on th' first level in th' clothin' exhibits. I was just finishin' cleanin' th' glass on the exhibit of Persian shoes."

"Oh yes," Felicia said. "I remember now seeing you there. You also had a broom and a dustpan with you. Isn't that right?"

Mr. Billings dipped his chin. "Yeah, I was just waiting for you two t' leave and then I was goin' to do a final cleaning of the 'ole floor."

"How long have you been working as a caretaker, Mr. Billings?" Ginger asked.

"Well, I bin 'ere for about five months now, I s'pose. Before that I was workin' as a caretaker in different schools an' 'ospitals. I'm the bloke 'oo can fix just about anythin' that goes wrong and can clean up a mess as good as you please. I'm as good wiv a bucket and mop as I am wiv a spanner. I s'pose I've been doin' this kind of work most of my life, even before the war."

"Is this the first time you have worked at a museum?"

"Yes, that's right I s'pose."

"Have you ever been in the vault where the valuables are being kept?"

"No one is allowed in there 'cept Mr. Hammond 'isself or Mr. Steadman, madam. I 'ave never seen the inside of it, I don't know wots there, and I don't 'ave a key."

"Thank you, Mr. Billings. That will be all for now. Please call in Mr. Barnes."

Mr. Billings gathered up his items and left the room. Ginger turned to Felicia.

"He has a strong alibi. We would have seen him leave the floor, since it was completely dark and he would have had to use a torch."

"Agreed." said Felicia. "So motive is very unlikely as well."

"I doubt he has the kind of connections one needs to fence this 'Blade of T'Abriz'. Though," Ginger added, "he may be a good actor. We don't know that he didn't just lie about his benign employment history."

Mr. Barnes' pockets did not reveal anything suspicious

either. He sat down nervously. "I don't mind saying that this is highly irregular."

"We don't like this any more than you do, Mr. Barnes," Ginger said. "You seem a bit agitated."

Mr. Barnes stared at both Ginger and Felicia with dark, questioning eyes, and then glanced away. If anyone looked suspicious, it was this man, Ginger thought.

"Oh, I am well enough," Mr. Barnes said, sounding defensive. "I just don't like being kept here like a prisoner, as if I'm a suspect. I've done nothing wrong."

"You do recognise that under the circumstances, we have to proceed with diligence," Ginger said. "If you have nothing to hide, then you have nothing to be concerned about. This should be all over soon."

"I hope you're right, Mrs. Reed. But it is highly irregular."

"I agree. Now, where were you at the moment the lights went off?"

"Truth be told, I was making use of the lavatory." Mr. Barnes shifted his shoulders back. "And I must tell you it took me a while to find my way out. I didn't have a torch with me and the place was pitch black. I even stumbled and fell, bumping my head on the corner of the washbasin as I went down." At this he lifted up some of his hair to reveal a large lump and a small cut on his left temple.

"Would we find blood on the washbasin there?" Felicia asked.

"I suppose you would. I haven't had a chance to go and clean it up yet."

Felicia made a note and then got up without a word to go to the public water closet, which was on the ground floor, not far from the office where they were meeting.

Mr. Barnes watched her leave, and Ginger watched him for a reaction. There was none.

"In any case," Mr. Barnes said, "after I got myself sorted and found the door, I tried to feel my way around. Then I saw someone crossing the main lobby with a torch in his hands, I think it was Mr. Steadman. Saw him climb the steps to the first level and a few seconds later the lights came on."

"Yes, that's when we saw him too," Ginger said. "He came up to make sure we were all right. Can I ask when you were taken on at the museum?"

"I've been working here since the beginning of this month, three weeks ago."

"Where did you work before that?"

"I don't see how that has anything to do with all of this," Mr. Barnes said with a hint of belligerence. Boss' head darted up and he emitted a soft whine. Ginger eyed him with a stern look of authority.

Mr. Barnes relented. "Before this, I worked as a caretaker at a school in Portsmouth, and before that at a hospital in Brentford. The school shut down a few months ago. That's why I applied here."

Felicia returned and nodded to Ginger, "There's a little bit of fresh blood on the washbasin and on the floor. Not a lot but it definitely looks like someone fell there."

Mr. Barnes huffed with an air of self-righteousness. "Can I go now?"

"Just one more question," Ginger said. "Did you know about the 'Blade of T'Abriz' and that it was stored in the vault in the basement?"

"No, I didn't. I mean to say that I did know that most of the newer artefacts are stored there in preparation for the forthcoming new exhibition, but I didn't have any knowledge of any bejewelled Persian dagger. I had never heard of it before Mr. Hammond announced it just now in the lounge."

Ginger blinked once and said, "Very well, Mr. Barnes, that is all for now. Thank you very much for your cooperation. You may join the others. We should have finished with all of this soon. Please call on Miss Greene, if you would, and ask her to bring her handbag." Mr. Barnes left the room.

"Well, well," said Ginger deep in thought.

"What's the matter?" asked Felicia.

"He said he hadn't even heard about the Blade of T'Abriz until we were in the lounge."

"Yes, that's right."

"Neither Mr. Hammond nor I have indicated that the stolen artefact was a Persian dagger, nor that it was bejewelled. It could just as easily be an unadorned sword. Yet Mr. Barnes just mentioned it after telling us he had never heard of the Blade of T'Abriz. The man is lying."

5

*F*elicia worked her lipstick-laden lips and squinted at Ginger. "But his alibi is very good."

"Yes," Ginger said, "I know, and yet he is hiding something. The injury he claimed may have happened earlier."

There was a soft knock, and the door to Mr. Hammond's office opened. "I say, I think I am next."

"Yes, Miss Greene, do please sit down."

Miss Greene was an attractive lady in her mid-twenties with clear skin, green eyes, dark hair, and a trim figure.

"I am afraid we have to ask you to empty your handbag," Ginger said. "You understand."

"Of course." Miss Greene emptied the contents onto the desk. Again, there was nothing suspicious about anything that she carried. After Felicia had finished writing down the contents, Miss Greene returned them to the bag.

"Can you please tell us what you were doing exactly when the lights went out?" Ginger asked.

"I was exactly where I usually am, working in my office."

"Was anyone with you?"

"No, I was alone. I daresay that makes me a bit more

suspect," said Miss Greene. Her mouth was turned up at one side in a sort of sardonic smile.

"It's a perfectly logical answer, Miss Greene."

Miss Greene leaned forward in her chair. "Isn't it a bit unusual that a lady is working as a private detective?"

"You're very direct." Ginger said smoothly. "Yes, it is, I suppose. Did you stay in your office while waiting for the lights to come back on?"

"Oh," said Miss Greene as if she was surprised Ginger didn't want to talk about her detective work. She leaned back in her chair. "Yes, I stayed at my desk and had a cigarette. I knew one of the men would get to the problem in good time."

"Now, you were the first employee that Mr. Hammond took on, is that correct?" Ginger asked.

"Yes."

"And before that you worked at a museum in Wales," Ginger said, consulting her notes.

"Yes. The Museum of Roman History in Cardiff. I was there three years before the museum was closed down. Lack of funding, sadly."

"And you helped interview the other job applicants?" Felicia asked.

"That's correct."

Felicia continued, "And was Mr. Steadman the first person you employed?"

Ginger looked at Felicia. Was she following a hunch?

"I am not sure that has anything to do with all of this," Miss Greene replied, "but yes, I suppose he was."

Ginger noted the defensiveness in her voice.

"He was taken on about two weeks after I got here."

"Did you know any of the applicants before they were taken on?" pressed Felicia.

"They each applied for the job the same as anyone," Miss Greene said indignantly, "by reading about it in the newspaper job postings."

"That's not what she asked," Ginger said. "Were you personally acquainted with any of them?"

"No, I was not."

"How much do you know about the Blade of T'Abriz?" Ginger asked.

"Mr. Hammond was quite secretive about what was in the vault. I think that was for security purposes," Miss Greene said. "He keeps written records of course, but I have never seen them and I know very little about Persian daggers or sapphires."

"How did you know it was a dagger and not a sword?" said Ginger. "And no one has mentioned anything about sapphires."

"Well I... I don't know, I just supposed," Miss Greene stammered. "When Mr. Hammond said it was called 'The Blade of T'Abriz', my mind just went to a bejewelled dagger, but I suppose from the name of it, it could be a sword."

"How do you like working here?" Ginger asked, letting the question about sapphires go unanswered.

"Oh, it's all right." Miss Greene paused for a moment. "But I am sure you know how it is, Mrs. Reed. Sometimes I feel like the place could be run a little better."

"I'm afraid I don't know what you mean," Ginger said.

"Well, being a woman who knows her mind like you do, I am sure you have worked with men who can't seem to take advice from members of the opposite sex. I mean, Mr. Hammond does an adequate job, but he's not one for details. Why, today's incident simply underscores that, doesn't it? I have suggested to him on several occasions that we find a more secure way to store the more valuable antiquities, but he's ignored my advice and, well... here we are, aren't we?"

"More secure than a locked vault?" Felicia said.

"It's a *padlock*."

"What advice would you have given him?" Ginger asked.

"Oh, I don't know." Miss Greene crossed her legs and the

top one swung. "Perhaps more than one lock on the door. Storing the artefacts in several rooms instead of all in one. We have several rooms down there that are empty now which could serve that purpose. Practical things like that."

"You seem to know a bit about how things are stored," Ginger commented.

"Oh, no, just in general terms. I've actually only been down there on one or two occasions." Her chin jerked up and she stared at Ginger. "But I have never been in the vault, of course."

"We thank you for your help, Miss Greene," Ginger said. "Please call in Mr. Steadman, will you?"

When Miss Greene left the room, Ginger said, "Another person who's veering from the truth."

"Yes," Felicia said. "And not just about the missing dagger."

"What do you mean?"

"It's just a hunch. I need to think about it some more."

"Very well," Ginger said. "We'll soon find out what Mr. Steadman has to say. He's the only other person who had a key to both the building and to the vault, and yet is the man who seems to have the most solid alibi."

6

*A*fter the usual emptying of the pockets, Mr. Steadman sat down in an empty chair. Ginger picked up the small key ring with two keys which the second curator had deposited on the desk.

"One is for the front door and one is for the vault," he said. One of the keys was a cast iron skeleton key normally used for exterior doors. Ginger held it up and could see nominal signs of wear. The other was a padlock key which looked virtually unused and fresh from the locksmith.

"So far I have only used the vault key twice," Mr. Steadman offered. "Once when I opened up the vault for the delivery lorry men to deliver the crates, and then again to close the door when they had finished later that same day. Other than that, I have never been in the vault."

"Were you there in the room as the delivery men unloaded the crates?" Ginger asked.

"No. Mr. Hammond had me doing other duties while the men were here."

"We already know where you were when the lights went out," Felicia said.

"Mr. Hammond and I each grabbed a torch, and he went

down to the fuse room while I went to the displays on the ground level here to make sure everyone was all right and to tell them to stay put. Then I went to the first floor to do the same. That's when the lights came back on. I went directly back to Mr. Hammond's office after that." This story matched perfectly with Mr. Hammond's account and also with what Ginger and Felicia had witnessed.

"Can you tell me where you worked before you came here to the Wainwright Museum?" Ginger asked.

"I worked at the Museum of Art and Literature in Berkshire as second curator for five years before it closed. Before that I worked at the Regimental Museum in Cornwall as a caretaker."

"So, you have quite a lot of experience at museums," Ginger said. It explained why Mr. Hammond had him as his right-hand man. "Have you ever had anything like this happen before in your career at museums?"

"No, never," he said simply.

"Are you married?" asked Felicia. Again Ginger considered her sister-in-law. She'd been asking a lot of seemingly random questions.

"I have never married, miss."

"Did you know anyone here before you came to work for the museum?" Felicia asked.

Mr. Steadman blinked, shifted slightly in his chair, and shook his head. "No, miss, I didn't know anyone."

"Very well, I think that's all for now," Ginger said. "Please go back to the lounge and let them know we will be there to join them shortly."

After Mr. Steadman left the room Ginger said, "Let's go over what we know so far, keeping in mind that we are looking at motive, means, and opportunity. We should rule out Mr. Hammond for the moment, he is lacking a motive, and has a lot to lose if this dagger isn't found soon.

"This means we have four suspects. Of those four, Mr.

Billings seems the most unlikely due to a solid alibi and lack of any real experience in the museum world, let alone having the kind of connections one needs to sell stolen artefacts."

"I agree," Felicia said.

Boss nudged Ginger's leg and she gave him permission to jump onto her lap. She stroked his head as she continued her recitation. "Then we have Mr. Barnes, who also has a very strong alibi due to the blood on the basin in the lavatory. It is not easy to fake something like that, if indeed, the blood belongs to him, and if the timing of his injury lines up."

Ginger's hand had stilled and Boss nosed it gently to remind her to keep up the stroking of his fur. Ginger's fingers responded as she continued. "Then we have Mr. Steadman who has the 'means', and he's the only one we know of who has a key. However, his alibi is the strongest of them all.

"And then there is Miss Greene who has the weakest alibi and is also lying about her knowledge of the dagger."

"That's not all she's lying about," Felicia added with a slight tilt to her head and a twinkle in her eye.

"What do you mean?" said Ginger in surprise.

"She and Mr. Steadman knew each other personally before they came to work here," Felicia said triumphantly. "I suspect they were, and still are, lovers."

7

*G*inger was quite taken aback by Felicia's pronouncement. "Why on earth would you say that?"

"It took me a while to piece it all together," started Felicia carefully. "Two of the suspects, Miss Greene and Mr. Steadman, looked strangely familiar, as if I'd seen them somewhere else before, but I couldn't quite place them. Then, when Miss Greene came in here for the interview and I heard her voice and her brash manner, I suddenly remembered!"

"Do tell," Ginger said, leaning in. This must have been the reason for Felicia's strange line of questioning.

"Last season, I was with a friend having some drinks down at that new flappers' jazz club in Mayfair. We were enjoying the music when we overheard a loud conversation at the next table. At that time we couldn't see who it was because of a large potted plant between the two tables, but it was impossible not to hear some of the conversation, which was clearly between a young lady and a man. She was berating him whilst he was trying to explain something. It was hard for him to get a word in!" Felicia's eyes widened and she shook her head as she said this, obviously mortified at the thought. "The conversation revolved around the fact that she thought he was being a bit of a milksop and that he didn't stand up for himself enough. She said that it looked like it was all up to her to make sure his talents were recognised by employers. I mostly only heard her end of the conversation since she was by far the loudest.

"Honestly, Ginger, we didn't mean to listen in, and at the time, I wished they would just leave. I don't know where some people get their manners. It is a very nice club, with some great musicians coming in from France and even America. Just last week there was a trio from New Orleans that was…"

"Did you meet them or talk to them?" Ginger interrupted. Felicia sometimes tended to wander off the topic.

"What? Oh, you mean the couple? Oh heavens, no, but they did make a bit of a grand exit. As they stood up, she started complaining loudly about the service in the club and the quality of the cocktails. That whole section of the club was quite outraged. But I got a very good view of both of them as they walked out. No doubt about it, it was our Miss Greene and Mr. Steadman. And not only that—"

"Come along. We need to search Miss Greene's office straightaway without alerting her that we are onto her."

"Do you think she is the thief? What could be her motive?"

"I don't know exactly what her game is, but I am beginning to get a picture."

Ginger, with Boss at her heels, and Felicia walked quickly to the second level to again face the suspects. They were all sitting in the exact seats they were before, smoking cigarettes and sipping tea.

"It's time we made a general search of the building," Ginger announced. "If we don't find anything, it may be time to bring the police into the matter. However, it would be best for the continuation of this museum, and thus for all of your jobs, if we could quickly settle this matter before the police have to step in and the whole affair becomes known to the press."

"You don't think that the thief is one of us, do you?" said Mr. Barnes.

"I think that's wot makes th' most sense at the moment," offered Mr. Billings. "Don't you?"

The staff shot looks of distrust at one another.

"I am not making any pronouncements at the moment," Ginger said. "And I thank you very much for your patience. Now, I propose we break into three teams. Mr. Hammond will go with Mr. Billings and Miss Greene whilst Miss Gold can go with Mr. Steadman and I'll go with Mr. Barnes."

Ginger wanted to have either Felicia, herself, or Mr. Hammond on each of the teams so the thief would be under the eye of someone who was sure to be objective and could ensure that no one pocketed the dagger if they happened upon it. Ginger chose to pair up with Mr. Barnes since, out of all the suspects, he was the one who seemed to be the most unpredictable based on his general personality and the fact that he was obviously lying about his background.

There was a murmur of agreement as everyone rose to their feet. "The cellar can be searched last after we have finished with the rest of the building," Ginger instructed, "but to begin, Mr. Barnes and I will search the ground floor. Mr. Hammond, would you be so kind as to lead your team onto the floor above us where the new exhibition is to open, and Felicia, you and Mr. Steadman can search this floor. We shall report back here in half an hour. If the dagger is still here, it will probably be hidden in an out-of-the-way spot, so look in every nook and cranny. It will also likely be wrapped in something or hidden in a small box of some kind. Keep in mind that after we come back from our searches we will empty our pockets again onto this table as a precaution."

Ginger, with Boss trotting along at her feet, headed

straight to Miss Greene's office which was on the ground floor and situated just around the corner from Mr. Hammond's larger office. Mr. Barnes followed close behind. Smelling faintly of cigarettes and oiled wood, Miss Greene's office was also tastefully decorated and very neat and tidy, with one window looking out over the front grounds. It contained a large wooden cabinet, two potted plants, and a large mahogany desk with a wooden chair. On the desk were some files and a large metal paperweight formed into the shape of a knight chess piece. There were also two unopened narrow cabinets. One of the doors of the big cabinet was not quite shut all the way, revealing a shoe rack and shelves filled with sundry items and small boxes that Ginger planned to search through.

"I'll start with the desk area, Mr. Barnes, if you would like to begin in the cabinets." Ginger opened the first drawer of the desk and sifted through the contents. There were six drawers in all, and she took her time sorting through the papers and assorted office items, keeping in mind that the dagger would likely be wrapped in some sort of cloth or pouch. From where she sat, Ginger could easily see Mr. Barnes at work, and she kept one eye on him whilst she searched the desk.

She had reached the bottom drawer of the desk when Boss whined, getting her attention. She looked up to see Mr. Barnes on his knees, staring blankly into the cabinet. "What is it?" she said as she walked to him. Mr. Barnes had cleared away the shoe rack and removed a small panel which served as a false wall. This uncovered a hidden compartment with a combination padlock on the small door.

"Mr. Barnes, could you please quickly return to the lounge, gathering my sister-in-law and Mr. Steadman on your way. I will go to the top floor to fetch Miss Greene. I will meet you in the lounge after we open this door. There might be nothing in here, but certainly Miss Greene has a reason for hiding it."

They both left the room and climbed the first staircase after which Mr. Barnes went left and Ginger walked to the next stairwell. It took several minutes to find Miss Greene who was in the middle of searching a chest of drawers next to a partially erected exhibit. Mr. Billings and Mr. Hammond were busy searching just down the hall.

"Please come with me, Miss Greene," Ginger instructed. When Miss Greene saw the determination in Ginger's eyes, her face went white. She nodded blankly and without a word slowly turned to follow Ginger. When they met up with the men in the corridor, Ginger said, "Mr. Billings, please join the others in the lounge. Mr. Hammond, please come with me and Miss Greene." The tone of her voice made everyone stop.

"Of course," Mr. Hammond said, and quickly walked towards Ginger.

Ginger, Mr. Hammond, and Miss Greene descended the two staircases without speaking and entered Miss Greene's office. Ginger stopped just inside the doorway.

"Good Lord!" Mr. Hammond said, as Miss Greene's hand flew to her mouth. The small padlocked door had been smashed open, and the compartment had clearly been emptied. The heavy chess-knight-shaped paperweight was on the floor beside the cupboard.

"Barnes," Ginger said.

8

"*I*t's time to alert the police," Ginger said.

Mr. Hammond's face had drained of colour. "There's no way out of here without a key."

"Are you sure there are no access doors or windows anywhere that open to the outside?" Ginger asked.

Mr. Hammond shook his head wearily. "None that I am aware of. The windows have all been permanently bolted shut for security."

"Good, then it's just a matter of the police searching the building. This may all be over very soon without making so much as a peep to the press, Mr. Hammond." Ginger turned to go.

Mr. Hammond called after her. "Wait! Now that I think of it, there is a high window in one of the cleaning supply rooms on this floor that does partially swing open. It's very hard to reach, but I imagine if one stacked some boxes or had a ladder one could manage it. A desperate man who was slim enough might fit through. It would be a rather far jump down to the grass, but I suppose…"

"Mr. Barnes is as slim as a toothpick, and I don't doubt

that some men would jump off the Tower of London if there was money to be made," Ginger said.

They ran to the supply room, which was located near Miss Greene's office, Boss' nails clicking over the floors behind them. The door was open and a ladder leaned against the wall under the small window which was left open to the outside.

Ginger immediately turned and ran to the front hall with Mr. Hammond alongside her, fumbling for his keys. He turned the key in the lock, and the large oak doors opened with a very loud creak. They stepped outside into the evening air to see Mr. Barnes sitting dejectedly on a bench, his hands cuffed behind his back. Two constables dressed in plain clothes were standing beside him with one of them scribbling in a notepad.

"Good evening, Mrs. Reed. Beautiful evening, isn't it?"

Ginger recognised the young and charming officer.

"It certainly is, Constable Braxton."

He drew close to Ginger and Mr. Hammond, and out of his pocket he pulled a large white handkerchief which he unrolled to reveal an ornately decorated dagger with a golden, jewel-encrusted hilt and a red velvet sheath.

THEY CELEBRATED LATER with Basil at Hartigan House over drinks. Ginger had asked Basil to bring Constable Braxton, not only to commend the young constable for his role in apprehending the thief, but as a treat for Felicia in reward for hers. Felicia had made herself cosy on the settee, rather near to the blushing constable.

Basil, wearing a crisp thin-collared shirt tucked into blue pinstripe trousers, sat with one leg crossing the knee of the other. A patterned wool-cashmere sock peeked out from between the folded cuff and his polished leather Italian shoes. He lifted his glass of sherry. "Good work to all of you!"

Ginger lifted her glass in return. "Thank you, love." She never tired of her husband's praises, and was well aware that their particular partnership was rare indeed. Basil's handsome hazel eyes glinted with pride as he grinned in that dapper manner she adored.

Basil broke their locked gaze to address the room. "It turns out our Mr. Barnes had several aliases, and had assumed one of the false identities to gain the job at the museum. He's a professional thief with a history of selling stolen jewellery to unscrupulous private collectors in France and Switzerland. He had designs on somehow stealing the dagger. He must have had a peek at Mr. Hammond's master list of vault contents that unfortunately was left unlocked in the main office. His plan though, was to wait for it to first go on display." He chuckled. "Unfortunately for him, Miss Greene beat him to it."

Basil continued, "Miss Greene has confessed to stealing the dagger using a key that she had made a copy of. It was a simple thing for her to steal the key from her unsuspecting lover, Mr. Steadman, and place it back in his belongings after she had the new key cut."

"Good gracious!" Felicia spouted. "Such deviousness."

"Indeed," Constable Braxton said. "What a nerve."

"Apparently Miss Greene and Steadman have been lovers for years," Basil said, "but the couple did not want to divulge that fact because it would obviously prohibit the employing of Mr. Steadman in the job of second curator."

"And let me guess her motive for stealing the dagger," said Ginger. Basil smiled and nodded.

"She didn't want to keep the dagger or steal it. That's the job of professional thieves who have the connections and experience to sell valuable antiquities off. Instead, she had planned to secretly 'misplace' the dagger, which would have eventually led to the end of Mr. Hammond's position at the

Wainwright Museum and possibly his career as well. Especially when the dagger was 'found' by his unsuspecting right-hand man, Mr. Steadman, who because of his background in museum work would likely have then been considered for the vacant position of head curator."

"Excellent guess," said Basil with a grin. "Miss Greene has made a full confession and denies Steadman had anything to do with it. Indeed, we have no proof that he did either. It seems Miss Greene was acting totally on her own without Steadman's knowledge. It was a simple thing for her to go down to where the electrical box was and slightly unscrew the appropriate fuses, plunging the building into darkness. It was also very clever of her to have that little hidden compartment in her cupboard. It was really just a small, lockable box which you can buy at any supply shop. She had modified the cabinet slightly to hide the box behind a false partition. She must have done it during office hours with her door closed. Ultimately a clever, although misguided, plan to further the career of her lover."

"What about you, Boss?" Ginger said. Boss jumped onto her lap and expectantly stared at her with his big brown eyes.

"After this case, perhaps he deserves a promotion," said Felicia. "We would never have solved this if he hadn't 'guided' us to the vault."

"Boss is more easily satisfied, I think." Ginger offered a piece of dried pig's ear she'd been saving in her handkerchief. "There, that usually does it."

They all laughed at the sight of Boss, the detective Boston terrier, happily devouring his favourite treat.

It's never too early to think about Christmas!
Ginger Gold's *Murder by Plum Pudding* is part of a multi-

author boxed set releasing in October. Preorders are available on Barnes & Noble, Apple Books, Kobo and Amazon. Get your preorder copy for only .99.

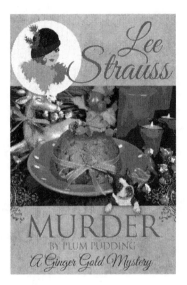

MURDER BY PLUM PUDDING

There's nothing more fun than a festive holiday dinner party and Ginger Reed, the former Lady Gold, has Hartigan House decorated and the gramophone playing. Dressed in her finest Parisian low-waisted gown, feather-topped tiara, and T-strapped Italian leather shoes, Ginger is ready to host the delectable event.

It's a jolly good time, until someone chokes on the *pudding*.

Is it an accident or is it murder? And can Ginger unravel the mystery before the church bells ring and the New Year's day dawns?

Click HERE to Preorder this special Christmas bundle

offer today! Only .99 - the price will go up when it releases individually.

WANT MORE GINGER GOLD?

Get Lady Gold Investigates Volume THREE - *The Case of Missing Time* and *The Case of the Unlucky Cricketeer.*

Murder on Eaton Square
The Ginger Gold Mysteries Book # 10

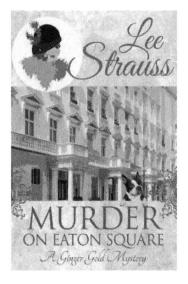

Did you know that Ginger kept a Journal?

Sign up for Lee's newsletter to get access to this exclusive content. Find out about Ginger's Life before the SS *Rosa* and how she became the woman she has. This is a fluid document that will cover her romance with her late husband Daniel, her time serving in the British secret service during World War One, and beyond. Includes a recipe for Dark Dutch Chocolate Cake!

Read on to learn more!

Join GINGER GOLD'S BOOK CLUB

Discuss the books, ask questions, share your opinions. Fun giveaways! Join the Lee Strauss Readers' Group on Facebook for more info.

Love the fashions of the 1920s? Check out Ginger Gold's Pinterest Board!

Join my Facebook readers group for fun discussions and first-to-know exclusives!

www.leestraussbooks.com

GINGER GOLD'S JOURNAL

Sign up for Lee's readers list and gain access to **Ginger Gold's private Journal.** Find out about Ginger's Life before the SS *Rosa* and how she became the woman she has. This is a fluid document that will cover her romance with her late husband Daniel, her time serving in the British secret service during World War One, and beyond. Includes a recipe for Dark Dutch Chocolate Cake!

It begins: **July 31, 1912**

How fabulous that I found this Journal today, hidden in the bottom of my wardrobe. Good old Pippins, our English butler in London, gave it to me as a parting gift when Father whisked me away on our American adventure so he could marry Sally. Pips said it was for me to record my new adventures. I'm ashamed I never even penned one word before today. I think I was just too sad.

This old leather-bound journal takes me back to that emotional time. I had shed enough tears to fill the ocean and I remember telling Father dramatically that I was certain to cause flooding to match God's. At eight years old I was well-trained in my biblical studies, though, in retro-spect, I would say that I had probably bordered on heresy with my little tantrum.

The first week of my "adventure" was spent with a tummy ache and a number of embarrassing sessions that involved a bucket and Father holding back my long hair so I wouldn't soil it with vomit.

I certainly felt that I was being punished for some reason. Hartigan House—though large and sometimes lonely—was my home and Pips was my good friend. He often helped me to pass the time with games of I Spy and Xs and Os.

"Very good, Little Miss," he'd say with a twinkle in his blue eyes when I won, which I did often. I suspect now that our good butler wasn't beyond letting me win even when unmerited.

Father had got it into his silly head that I needed a mother, but I think the truth was he wanted a wife. Sally, a woman half my father's age, turned out to be a sufficient wife in the end, but I could never claim her as a mother.

Well, Pips, I'm sure you'd be happy to know that things turned out all right here in America.

SUBSCRIBE to read more!
www.leestraussbooks.com

.

ABOUT THE AUTHORS

Lee Strauss is the bestselling author of The Ginger Gold Mysteries series, The Higgins & Hawke Mystery series (cozy historical mysteries), A Nursery Rhyme Mystery series (mystery suspense), The Perception series (young adult dystopian), The Light & Love series (sweet romance), and young adult historical fiction with over a million books read. She has titles published in German, Spanish and Korean, and a growing audio library. She also writes younger YA fantasy as Elle Lee Strauss.

Norm Strauss is a singer-songwriter and performing artist who's seen the stage of The Voice of Germany. Short story writing is a new passion he shares with his wife Lee Strauss.

For more info on books by Lee Strauss and her social media links, visit leestraussbooks.com. To make sure you don't miss the next new release, be sure to sign up for her readers' list!

Did you know you can follow your favourite authors on Bookbub? If you subscribe to Bookbub — (and if you don't, why don't you? - They'll send you daily emails alerting you to sales and new releases on just the kind of books you like to read!) — follow me to make sure you don't miss the next Ginger Gold Mystery!

BB Follow on BookBub

www.leestraussbooks.com
leestraussbooks@gmail.com

BOOKS BY LEE STRAUSS

On AMAZON

Ginger Gold Mysteries (cozy 1920s historical)

Cozy. Charming. Filled with Bright Young Things. This Jazz Age murder mystery will entertain and delight you with its 1920s flair and pizzazz!

Murder on the SS *Rosa*

Murder at Hartigan House

Murder at Bray Manor

Murder at Feathers & Flair

Murder at the Mortuary

Murder at Kensington Gardens

Murder at St. Georges Church

Murder Aboard the Flying Scotsman

Murder at the Boat Club

Murder on Eaton Square

Murder by Plum Pudding

Lady Gold Investigates (Ginger Gold companion short stories)

Volume 1

Volume 2

Volume 3

Higgins & Hawke Mysteries (cozy 1930s historical)

The 1930s meets Rizzoli & Isles in this friendship depression era cozy mystery series.

Death at the Tavern

Death on the Tower

Death on Hanover

A Nursery Rhyme Mystery (mystery/sci fi)

Marlow finds himself teamed up with intelligent and savvy Sage Farrell, a girl so far out of his league he feels blinded in her presence - literally - damned glasses! Together they work to find the identity of @gingerbreadman. Can they stop the killer before he strikes again?

Gingerbread Man

Life Is but a Dream

Hickory Dickory Dock

Twinkle Little Star

The Perception Trilogy (YA dystopian mystery)

Zoe Vanderveen is a GAP—a genetically altered person. She lives in the security of a walled city on prime water-front property along side other equally beautiful people with extended life spans. Her brother Liam is missing. Noah Brody, a boy on the outside, is the only one who can help ~ but can she trust him?

Perception

Volition

Contrition

Light & Love (sweet romance)

Set in the dazzling charm of Europe, follow Katja, Gabriella, Eva, Anna and Belle as they find strength, hope and love.

Sing me a Love Song

Your Love is Sweet

In Light of Us

Lying in Starlight

Playing with Matches (WW2 history/romance)

A sobering but hopeful journey about how one young Germany boy copes with the war and propaganda. Based on true events.

As Elle Lee Strauss

The Clockwise Collection (YA time travel romance)

Casey Donovan has issues: hair, height and uncontrollable trips to the 19th century! And now this ~ she's accidentally taken Nate Mackenzie, the cutest boy in the school, back in time. Awkward.

Clockwise

Clockwiser

Like Clockwork

Counter Clockwise

Clockwork Crazy

Standalones

Seaweed

Love, Tink

Library and Archives Canada Cataloguing in Publication Title: Lady Gold investigates : a short read cozy historical 1920s mystery collection / Lee Strauss. Names: Strauss, Lee (Novelist), author. Description: Short stories. | v. 2. The case of the recipe robbery -- The case of the museum heist. Identifiers: Canadiana (print) 20190131608 | Canadiana (ebook) 20190131624 | ISBN 9781774090480 (v. 2 ; IngramSpark softcover) | ISBN 9781774090466 (v. 2 ; softcover) | ISBN 9781774090473 (v. 2 ; hardcover) | ISBN 9781774090442 (v. 2 ; Kindle) | ISBN 9781774090459 (v. 2 ; EPUB) Classification: LCC PS8637.T739 L34 2019 | DDC C813/.6—dc23

Made in the USA
San Bernardino, CA
13 November 2019